ECHOES OF LOVE

Mauro Reolon

Table of Contents

To all the brave souls who dare to seek the truth within themselves, even when it means challenging everything they've ever known.

To those who surrender to love and pain with the same intensity, unafraid of getting lost in the process — knowing that only by losing ourselves do we find the true meaning of life.

To you, who chooses to live and begin again, who does not fear breaking free from the chains of the past to embrace what lies ahead, with the certainty that the journey is never in vain.

This book is for the hearts that still beat fiercely, even on the quietest nights — and for the eyes that still shine, even when the stars seem to have faded.

To those who dare to be whole, unafraid to be seen, unafraid to show themselves.

To all who seek the truth, wherever it may lead them.

And especially to my son and my wife, who supported me throughout this journey.

About the Author

Mauro is a psychologist and enthusiastic storyteller who delves into the complexities of human emotions and relationships. With his professional background in psychology and a deep understanding of the human soul, he crafts narratives that invite readers to explore desire, love, pain, and redemption.

Inspired by real-life stories and the transformative power of love, Mauro looks to connect with readers on an intimate level, offering reflections that resonate long after the last page is turned.

When he's not writing, Mauro enjoys cooking, music, and spending time with his family. He lives in London with his wife and son, where he continues to nurture his love for storytelling and emotional exploration.

PROLOGUE

In a world where feelings often get lost in the complexities of everyday life, Isadora's story is an invitation to dive deep into the realms of desire, pain, and redemption. It is a tale of inner transformation — of what happens when the masks fall, and human beings are confronted with their most primal and, at the same time, most intricate needs.

Isadora, a woman with an intense soul and emotions worn on her sleeve, finds herself on the edge of an emotional storm that challenges her own beliefs and values. Married to Daniel, a man who loved her deeply, she nonetheless finds herself in a space where love is no longer enough to fill the voids she carries inside. The desire to be seen, to be desired, becomes a flame that consumes her — making her question her identity and the role she plays in Daniel's life.

Their marriage, marked by highs and lows, becomes the backdrop for a journey of self-discovery, where the search for pleasure, for recognition, and for truth intertwines with the pain of limitation and unfulfilled longing. When a new world opens before Isadora, she finds herself at a crossroads: to follow the rules of what she knows or to leap into the unknown, where freedom and pleasure promise a new form of happiness.

This book is not merely about love or sex but about the boundaries of the human soul. It is about the choices we make and how those choices define who we are — even when their weight seems unbearable. With each page, you will be invited to question your own limits, to look inward, and to reflect on what it truly means to live a life of authenticity — without masks, without embellishments.

At its core, this is a story about what it means to be human: imperfect, complex, and, above all, free to choose one's own path —

even if that path brings pain, pleasure, and the scars of a journey that is difficult but necessary.

Isadora's story is the story of all of us. Of our internal struggles, of the desires that shape us, and of the consequences of our decisions. As you allow yourself to enter this universe, you may discover something about yourself. Like Isadora, you, too, will allow yourself to rediscover who you are — in the most intimate and profound moment of your existence.

Prepare for a journey without filters, without restraints.

Where what lies hidden in the heart is revealed, and what seems irreversible may, in truth, be transformed.

Welcome to Isadora's journey.

CHAPTER 1
THE SEED OF RESTLESSNESS

The wind blew fiercely across the fields, carrying with it the scent of wet earth and memories that would never fade.

It was there, in the forgotten countryside of the world, that Isadora was born — the daughter of broken promises and abandoned dreams.

Her father and mother vanished like summer storms: swift, violent, leaving behind only destruction.

Still a baby, she was handed over to the austere arms of her grandmother Áurea, a woman of few words and feelings locked away behind seven keys.

The baby's cries pierced the dawn like an ancient, ancestral lament. On the doorstep of the modest house, under the dim light of a kerosene lamp, Áurea clutched the doorframe as if it could hold her upright against what her eyes refused to accept.

Before her stood her daughter — thin, eyes hollow with fear — holding Isadora wrapped in a faded blanket. Behind her, the young man stared at the ground, hands in his pockets, his soul crushed by guilt.

"I... I can't, Mama," the young woman said, her voice trembling. "I tried. But I just can't. She cries all the time, doesn't sleep, I don't sleep... Felipe can't find work, we're starving. I don't know what to do anymore..."

Felipe squeezed his eyes shut, bit his lip, and swallowed the words burning in his throat. He loved that child too — but love, alone, was a runaway horse on a minefield. He had tried selling fruit at the market working in the fields, but every coin seemed to vanish like smoke, and every night was a new nightmare. When Isadora fell ill, they looked at each other and knew they wouldn't make it alone.

Áurea said nothing. She simply extended her arms and took the baby as if cradling fate itself. The child nestled into her chest, softly sobbing, unaware of everything breaking around her. The grandmother felt her heart silently shatter. It wasn't just the child being abandoned — it was also her daughter, her hope, the continuity of her story. She closed her eyes for a moment, like someone praying without faith, begging some unseen force to make her strong enough not to drown.

Isadora's mother turned her back too quickly. She couldn't bear to look at what she was leaving behind. But as she stepped off the porch, a small whimper from the baby made her stumble. She almost went back. Almost. But she didn't. Life was screaming her name with desperate pleas and promises too fragile to carry a child. Felipe wrapped his arm around her waist and whispered, "Let's go." And they went.

Inside the house, Áurea sat in the rocking chair — the same one she had once used to cradle her own daughter. She looked down at the child in her arms and felt a surge of love and despair she couldn't name. Silent tears traced lines across her stern face, carving paths where life had been harsher than time. She didn't hate her daughter. She didn't blame the boy. But at that moment, she hated the world for making such a tiny baby a burden to two broken youths.

Isadora, too young to understand abandonment, clenched her tiny fists against her chest and curled into the warmth of this new embrace. There was a different scent, a different heartbeat. But there was also something instinctive, ancestral, that slowly soothed her cries. Somehow, in a mysterious way, her soul seemed to know even in abandonment, there was love. And even in Áurea's silence, there was a promise of care.

That night, three people cried along different paths. Áurea, in her chair, rocking an uncertain future. The mother, lost on a bus, vanishing into the dust of the road, feeling her chest hollow out. And the father, walking silently beside her, holding back his tears like someone holding his breath to avoid drowning.

But one didn't cry: little Isadora, who fell asleep wrapped in arms that hadn't chosen her — but that would never let her fall.

Isadora's childhood was made of hot days, bare feet on the earth, and eyes lost on the horizon, searching for answers no one seemed willing to give.

Sometimes, alone in the backyard, she imagined being someone else — someone who shone before cameras, someone who lived under lights and applause, far from the dust and silence of the farm.

But dreams, no matter how distant, were seeds planted deep — and like all things in the soil, one day they would grow.

Áurea, though as tough as the cracked earth in August, never let her go without food, shelter, or school. She cared for Isadora with a silence that spoke louder than any advice. There were nights when the girl heard her grandmother weeping quietly in the next room — but she never had the courage to ask why. Instead, she learned to swallow her own tears.

At the village school, Isadora was the girl with beautiful words. Her essays made the teacher sigh, and she recited poems as if they were her own memories. Her classmates nicknamed her "the actress," laughing, unaware they were naming a deep yearning. She smiled in silence, accepting the nickname like a prophecy.

At thirteen, she secretly took her grandfather's old radio, buried among the junk in the shed, and began listening to soap operas and late-night shows, daydreaming about cities where no one knew her story. She imagined wide streets, lit-up theatres, and voices calling her name with respect and admiration.

And it was on one of those nights, lying on the roof of the house, gazing at a sky powdered with stars, that she made the promise that would change her life:

"One day, I'm leaving this place. Even if I must walk."

At sixteen, her world changed for the first time.

Lucas.

The name still burned sweetly in her memory.

The boy with rough hands and a shy smile. The one who, on a golden summer afternoon, stole her first kiss beneath the heavy branches of a mango tree.

With him, she discovered touch, warmth, and the feeling of being truly desired.

She gave herself to him without guilt, without fear — and unknowingly etched that sensation into her skin and soul forever.

Lucas was the first man who made her feel alive.

And in a way, he never stopped being.

But Isadora longed for more than young love hidden under the starry rural skies.

Her heart beat for something she barely understood: the desire to be seen, admired, recognized.

At eighteen, with little more than courage and a makeshift suitcase, Isadora left.

She left behind the farm, her grandmother, Lucas, and all the simplicity that had once sheltered — and imprisoned — her.

She climbed aboard the old bus that rumbled down the dusty road and, without looking back, headed to the big city in search of flashes, runways, and the life she had always believed she deserved.

What she didn't know yet was that the spotlight's glow would demand a steep price.

And that somewhere deep inside her, the farm girl still carried invisible scars — and desires that one day would break free from all restraints.

CHAPTER 2
BACK TO THE ORIGINS

The big city wasn't made of dreams — it was made of haste, of honking horns, of eyes that pierced through the body without ever truly touching it.

Isadora spent the first months lost between temporary jobs, small fashion shows, and failed attempts to break into the world she had always dreamed of.

Between one forced smile and another, she met a few men: empty promises, lukewarm kisses, touches that never set her skin ablaze the way Lucas once did in her memories.

No matter how hard she tried, no matter how desperately she sought new beginnings, there were nights when the past struck too hard inside her.

And on one of those nights, alone in her small rented room, longing took over.

It was a void that not even the city's false shine could fill.

Without much thought, she packed a few clothes, ran down the building stairs, and boarded the first bus heading back to the countryside.

For hours, the rhythm of the road brought every memory back: the scent of his skin, the heat of hidden kisses, the sweet weight of first times.

When she arrived in the old town, her heart beat erratically, like it had the first time she gave herself to him.

She knew where to find him — in the same place where the past still breathed.

Lucas now lived with another woman.

But when he saw her standing at the doorway of the small wooden house, his eyes were pure shock.

In seconds, the years disappeared.

Without a word, he pulled her inside, slamming the door behind them.

On the living room floor, he threw down an old mattress as if the entire universe had conspired to lead to that moment.

Isadora didn't think.

She didn't care.

The instant their bodies touched, the world ceased to exist.

He laid her down roughly, tearing the thin blouse she wore, kissing every inch of her skin with the desperate hunger of a man finding water in the middle of the desert.

His calloused hands gripped her waist, her thighs, and her face as if trying to hold onto the time that kept slipping away.

When he entered her — with raw brutality and aching need — she arched her body, moaning loudly, unashamed.

It was more than sex: it was a reunion, it was anger, it was ancient love that had never truly died.

Lucas took her as if she still belonged to him.

As if time, distance, and every mistake had never existed.

And there, on that forgotten mattress, Isadora understood a truth that would never leave her: some loves cut so deep that not even time, pride, or life itself can erase them.

That night, they belonged to each other.

Completely.

For the last time.

But before the end, there was more.

There were eyes locked together as he moved inside her as if searching for answers he didn't know how to ask aloud.

There was silence — thick, pulsing silence — in which every sigh was a confession, every touch a memory reborn.

He kissed her back slowly, like someone reading a sacred book, and Isadora closed her eyes, allowing herself to forget everything that stood between them.

She held his shoulders as if she could stop time as if in that fusion of skin and desire, there might be salvation.

When Lucas turned her on her side and pulled her tightly against him, he whispered her name like an apology, a silent plea.

She felt his body tremble, almost breaking, as he entered her again — now with less urgency, with more pain.

It was as if they were saying goodbye with their bodies because their hearts had never known how to do it.

The next moments were like diving without air: she moaned his name, biting the sheets, while he buried his face in her hair, trying to capture the scent, the taste, the warmth.

The climax came like a brutal, unstoppable wave, washing away everything: hurt, pride, reason.

They became one.

For the first time since goodbye.

And the last.

Afterwards, they lay side by side, breathless, sweating, in silence.

Their bodies still warm, their hearts at war.

Neither dared to speak of what would come next.

Isadora knew there was no future there. But in that moment, the past was the only place where she could breathe.

And there, in the silence after the storm, she understood: some loves don't end — they merely fall asleep inside us, waiting for the moment to wake again.

CHAPTER 3
PROMISES TO THE WIND
(EXPANDED VERSION)

Fate has strange — and often cruel — ways of changing a life.

Isadora would never have imagined that, after the boldness of returning to Lucas and the pain of leaving him behind once again, it would be in an industrial factory — surrounded by drills, worn-out uniforms, and deafening machines — that she would meet the man who, for a time, would give direction to her uncertain path.

His name was Daniel.

Tall, dark-skinned, his skin weathered by the sun and a tired gaze that seemed to have lived more than time should allow. There was an old sorrow in him but also a steadiness that made Isadora feel, for the first time in a long while, that she could trust someone again — even without knowing exactly why.

Daniel worked in the testing sector and, from the very first day, watched her from a distance — not with invasive eyes, but with a gaze that gently touched. When she walked past, sweaty and stained with grease, she felt his eyes on her like a warm breeze: silent yet undeniably present.

In time, they began sharing coffee during breaks, then shy laughter, and then silences that didn't feel awkward.

There was a curious peace in that unspoken companionship — a kind of mutual shelter built through small gestures: him saving her a piece of cake at lunch, her offering a painkiller when his forehead wrinkled with discomfort.

Their first kiss happened at a rodeo party, surrounded by country music, dust, and colourful lights. Isadora wore a borrowed blouse and painful shoes but forgot all of that when Daniel pulled her close by the waist and pressed his lips to hers — without asking, yet with the gentleness of someone who had once been wounded by love.

It was a kiss both urgent and tender, wet and full of something Isadora couldn't name — a mix of restrained desire and a promise of refuge.

Less than a month later, they were already sharing a tiny, rented apartment, a mattress on the floor, and a pile of unpaid bills. They had little — almost nothing — but Isadora felt less alone.

Bedtime conversations became a habit, laughter during showers, a survival ritual. Life, however, was not kind. The factory announced layoffs, and soon they were both out — unemployed, disoriented, scraping by with odd jobs, selling whatever they could, cooking plain rice with forced smiles.

Hunger hurt, but the lack of purpose hurt more. Still, she tried to believe it was just a phase.

It was Daniel who suggested they try their luck abroad.

A friend had found work in construction in a distant land — a place Isadora only knew from school maps.

"We can start over there," he said, with that look that blended hope and desperation.

She hesitated, but deep down, she knew the little they had was barely enough.

The goodbye was quick, stripped of poetry. Promises whispered through tears, old suitcases, and hugs that didn't want to let go.

Daniel left her at his mother's house — a quiet woman with dry hands and wary eyes.

"I'll come back for you in a few months," he promised. And she, heart clenched, believed him. Or wanted to.

The mother-in-law's house was cold — not because of the walls, but because of the silences.

The woman wasn't cruel, but neither was she welcoming. Her words were few, her movements cautious.

Isadora tried not to intrude, not to accept too much space. She had a small room, a hard bed, and the constant memory of Daniel hanging in the air.

She got a job at a shopping mall, selling clothes with a rehearsed smile and aching feet. The routine drained her, but she stayed strong.

Every night, when she returned home, she'd open the grimy window of her room and stare out at the empty street, imagining where Daniel might be.

What he might be eating. Whether he thought of her. If he missed her. If he still wanted her.

He called. Not often. Sometimes weeks would go by.

The calls were filled with static as if he were speaking from another planet, and the silences between sentences said more than any words could.

But Isadora clung to that voice — to those small anchors that, in some way, kept her heart tied to the promise of a future.

"I miss you, my love." "I'm waiting for you."

With what little she earned, she paid half the household bills, bought her own things, and still hid coins and bills in an envelope tucked inside an old book.

She called it her "turning-point money," though she didn't quite know what was supposed to turn.

Sometimes, she wrote letters to Daniel and never sent them.

She kept them in a shoebox, like confessions waiting for time itself to read on her behalf.

Daniel said the work was hard, the cold unbearable, and the boss unfair.

But he also said he was doing it for them — to build something.

"Just a few more months," he repeated. And she, even exhausted, even doubtful, would say: "I'm here."

But the truth was, there were days she didn't know where she was any more where she got lost.

Where his absence began and where her own disappearance ended.

Over time, something within Isadora began to shift.

A muted unrest, a longing to rediscover herself.

She missed recognizing her own reflection in the mirror.

She missed laughing freely, dancing on impulse, being looked at with desire — not through memories, but through real eyes.

She began putting on makeup even when she had nowhere to go.

She tried on old clothes as if searching for a forgotten version of herself.

There were nights when she dreamt of other cities, other lives.

She would wake up breathless, with the feeling that something was about to happen.

And then, on one of those ordinary mornings, while combing her hair in front of the cracked mirror in her room, Isadora realized something simple yet definitive:

She was no longer waiting.

Not out of anger. Not for revenge.

But by instinct.

Like someone who understands that certain promises are like leaves in the wind — beautiful while they dance but impossible to hold.

Isadora didn't tell anyone she had stopped waiting. It wasn't the kind of thing one announces. It was like a thread snapping inside her — no sound, no drama — just the quiet certainty that something had shifted. She began to walk differently as if she no longer carried an invisible weight on her back. Sometimes, she would smile to herself on a crowded bus as though she had rediscovered a forgotten piece of her own soul.

The envelope inside the old book was still there, but now she looked at it differently. No longer as a symbol of salvation but as a reminder that she could, indeed, choose another path. She started writing less to Daniel and more to herself. Loose phrases in old notebooks, thoughts scattered on grocery lists. Writing became a mirror — a place where she could exist without having to ask for space.

One ordinary afternoon at work, she received a message from an unknown number. It was Daniel. His voice was the same, but something had changed. A distance. A hesitation she didn't recognize. He spoke of hardship, of cold nights and long hours, but didn't ask much about her anymore. He didn't say he loved her. And when he mentioned it might take longer than expected to come back, Isadora simply replied, "I understand," — and for the first time, she didn't cry.

That night, she looked at herself in the mirror for a long time. There were dark circles under her eyes, fine lines she hadn't noticed before — but there was also a new kind of light behind them. A woman more tired, yes, but also more whole. She grabbed a pair of scissors and cut her own hair. No drama. No symbolism. Just the gesture of someone quietly starting over, inside and out.

Isadora didn't know exactly what would come next. But for the first time in a long while, she wasn't afraid. She didn't need promises or maps. Just the next step. And so, she fell asleep — not waiting for anyone but finally feeling like she was coming home to herself.

Chapter 4
Fragile Happiness

The reunion felt like a breath after months underwater.

Daniel came back.

Thinner, worn out, his gaze heavy with battles fought in faraway lands — and yet, his eyes still held the promise he had once made.

Isadora, though scarred by waiting, gave in. Love — or what remained of it — was enough to bring them together.

They married in a small ceremony — a few relatives, quiet flowers, trembling vows.

They left the country, holding hands, filled with hope.

For a while, they were happy.

They learned to walk side by side in a foreign land, where the language was different and solitude constant.

They built a modest home, warm and quiet, where love seemed enough to hold everything together.

But Daniel never truly returned.

He was there — under the same roof, sharing bills, filling the silences — yet absent in a way Isadora couldn't name.

Something vital was missing: the fire, the pulse of desire that sustains both body and soul.

From the beginning, intimacy between them was scarce.

Daniel tried. She pretended. But nothing reached the blaze that Lucas had once ignited in her.

There was a hunger — not just of the body, but of being seen — that Daniel could not touch.

And he noticed.

In her silence. In her far-off eyes. In her hesitant touch.

He responded with gentleness, with patience, with unspoken vows that they would make it work.

Their child's birth was the peak of their fragile joy.

Isadora surrendered to motherhood with a fierce love, discovering a new reason to exist.

But life, once again, had other trials in store.

Two years after the birth, Daniel began to change.

Doctors. Tests. Endless nights.

The diagnosis came like a sentence: a degenerative vascular condition that would permanently affect his ability to have erections.

What was once fragile became almost nonexistent.

And with it, the illusion of a passion that could still bloom began to crumble.

They tried to adjust.

Between diapers, unpaid bills, and sleepless nights, they looked for new ways to love.

Tenderness replaced desire. Guilt threaded their touches.

But deep down, she knew a part of her was crying out for something Daniel, no matter how much he loved her, could no longer give.

And there, in the stillness of night, rocking her child to sleep, Isadora felt a new hunger begin to stir.

Not just for sex.

For life.

To feel alive again.

Strangely, once she stopped fighting it, the days grew lighter.

Not easier — life still beat on with its rhythm of bills, long shifts, and silent dinners — but lighter, as if some hidden knot had finally loosened enough to let the air pass through.

Isadora began to notice the world in pieces again: the girl at the checkout humming softly, the old man feeding pigeons by the fountain, and the golden light entering the bus window at dusk.

Sometimes, she would sit alone on a bench, face turned toward the sun, eyes closed.

It wasn't joy — not yet — but something close, like the prelude to it.

In her notebook, she wrote phrases without much thought:

"There's a life whispering to me. I think I'm beginning to hear it."

Her relationship with Daniel didn't end in a rupture but in slow erosion.

No fights, no betrayal, no dramatic goodbye — just the gradual wearing down of a bond stretched too thin.

When he stopped seeking her, she took time to notice.

And when she did, she didn't panic.

A strange calm took hold — not indifference, but acceptance.

As if the end had happened long ago, and her heart was only now catching up.

One afternoon, while cleaning the store's back room, she found a dusty old Polaroid camera.

No one claimed it.

That weekend, she walked the city, taking pictures — of cracked windows in old buildings, of children chasing bubbles in the park, of her own shadow stretched across the pavement.

When she developed the photos, she laid them on her bed like relics from a life finally beginning to emerge.

Her room, once bare and silent, began to bloom.

She taped up photos, magazine clippings, and postcards from places she had never been.

Her walls became a small sanctuary — not of memories, but of promises.

Not from someone else but from herself to herself.

She laughed again.

First at Luana's crude jokes in the stockroom, then at her own reflection as she tried on silly hats just to make the others laugh.

Luana invited her to a community dance class.

She refused the first time. The second time, she went.

Clumsy, offbeat, sweating — but present.

Her body, stiff from routine and memory, began to recall the joy of movement.

That night, she returned home with aching feet and a smile she didn't try to hide.

She looked into the cracked mirror above the dresser and saw something awaken.

Not beauty. Not confidence.

Life.

And it startled her.

She didn't know how long she had been asleep.

That night, she slept deeply, dreamlessly, as if her soul had finally stopped holding its breath.

She didn't know exactly when she had stopped waiting for Daniel.

Maybe she hadn't stopped loving him — not entirely.

But now she understood: love could remain, quietly, in the corner of a story that was already moving on without him.

Perhaps she had folded that love gently like an old letter one no longer needs to read.

He would always be a part of her — but no longer the part that guided her.

What mattered now was something else:

The slow, quiet awakening of a woman finally learning to belong to herself.

CHAPTER 5
THE SILENT HUNGER

The nights became mirrors. In the reflection of the dark windows, Isadora saw a woman she barely recognized.

Hair hastily tied back, deep under-eye circles, milk-stained nightgowns — remnants of maternal love mixed with the ruins of a passion that had died in silence.

Daniel did what he could. He was kind, present, and attentive as far as his pain allowed. But he was not always understood — and many times, he strayed from the path. It wasn't all flowers. He had made his share of mistakes.

Still, something was broken between them. And no matter how much they tried to glue the pieces back together, what was once desired was now merely effort.

Isadora began walking.

At first, it was quick laps around the block, the baby in a stroller, headphones in her ears — escaping the routine with short steps.

Then came the online courses, the hidden books, and the dance videos watched at low volume while the baby slept.

Something inside her was moving — slowly, persistently — like water carving into stone.

One night, sitting on the living room floor after putting the baby to bed, she looked at her hands.

They were calloused but steady. They had built so much — and could still build more.

On her phone screen, an open tab showed an ad for a free theatre course at a community school across the city. Classes would start in two weeks. At night.

She knew Daniel wouldn't understand. That Grandma Áurea, in all her rural and emotional distance, would disapprove.

But for the first time in a long time, Isadora didn't want permission.

She wanted to try.

Not out of revenge. Not out of loneliness.

But because, in the midst of diapers and silence, of pain and waiting, she was still a woman.

And that woman — the one who dreamed of lights, of applause, of hearing her own voice echo on the stage of life — was still alive. Hungry.

And finally beginning to rise.

Daniel had always been an introspective man but not blind.

He noticed Isadora's subtle absences — the long gazes out the window, the smiles that no longer reached her eyes.

And though he never said it out loud, he felt the emptiness growing between them like a crack in concrete.

On a warm Wednesday night, while their son slept and the fan's soft hum filled the house, Daniel broke the silence:

— "Isa... can I ask you something?" His voice came out low, almost hesitant.

She, sitting at the foot of the bed with a book in her lap, just nodded.

— "I know that... things have changed between us. And I know you miss something that I... that I can't give you anymore." He took a deep breath. "But there's another way. A way... for you to still feel alive."

Isadora frowned, not understanding. He looked away for a moment, then locked eyes with hers, a mix of courage and pain.

— "Have you ever heard of... a threesome? But… only with another man."

She stared at him, stunned. There was something genuine in his voice — and something desperate, too.

An offer made not out of lust but out of love — or guilt.

— "You want to share me?" she whispered.

— "I don't want any of this, Isa. But I love you. And watching you wither away hurts more than anything. If this is a way for you to… reconnect with yourself, I can accept it. At least if it's someone we choose together. Carefully. With respect."

The book slipped from her hands, landing softly on the rug.

She didn't know whether to laugh or cry. She had never imagined hearing this from the man she shared such quiet nights and such tiny cribs with.

Inside her, shock wrestled with compassion. It wasn't a vulgar proposal.

It was a final gesture of surrender. A plea not to lose her completely.

She didn't answer that night.

She didn't know what to say.

But she knew, with painful clarity, that something between them had changed forever.

In the days that followed, Isadora carried a storm inside her she couldn't name.

She tried to keep up with the routine — coffee, diapers, grocery store, silence — but nothing felt the same.

Daniel's words repeated like a muffled echo, stirring feelings in her that ranged from disbelief to fear... and something she hesitated to admit: curiosity.

Daniel, for his part, seemed calmer like he had removed a weight from his chest.

On a rainy morning, while the baby napped in the stroller and the kettle whistled in the background, he brought it up again.

— "I know it sounds crazy, Isa. But... there's something I didn't tell you that night."

She looked up from the teapot, tense. He went on:

— "When I pictured you with another man... I felt something. Not just pain or jealousy. But... arousal. Desire." He swallowed hard as if confessing a dirty secret.

— "I started to think... maybe this, somehow, could spark something in me too."

Isadora stayed silent. Not out of disgust. Not from shock. But because, deep down, it made sense.

Daniel was trying to salvage the last scraps of desire between them.

Even if it meant taking a twisted path.

— "You want to see me with someone else?" she asked slowly.

— "I want to see you alive. Desired. Feeling pleasure. And if that brings me back... even a little, I think it's worth trying."

He shrugged, giving a half-hearted, bittersweet smile.

— "The illness affects my body, but desire... it's still here. Just trapped somewhere else."

That was the day he suggested they look for someone together.

— "A man who'll accept the rules. Who's discreet. Who understands that this... is about us. Not betrayal."

The idea still seemed absurd to Isadora — but she couldn't deny that something deep inside her had been awakened.

It wasn't just the invitation.

It was being seen. Desired.

Allowed.

The mirror that once reflected the mother, the wife, and the tired woman now showed cracks.

And through them appeared the shadow of a woman who might still be able to be reborn.

That same night, after they had put their son to sleep and the house had quieted down, Isadora sat beside Daniel on the bed, wrapped in a dense silence. She didn't say anything for a few minutes. She just looked at him for a long while.

There was something in his eyes—not just sadness or fear anymore.

It was desire. Raw, vulnerable, like someone offering a wound and asking it to be touched.

She turned off the bedside lamp. They were in the dark.

And it was in the dark that she decided to evaluate it.

She began with gentle touches as if reigniting a sleeping memory.

She kissed his neck and his shoulders and let the silence speak for her until the moment she brought her lips close to Daniel's ear and whispered:

— You know what I sometimes thought about when you couldn't anymore?

— What...? — he replied in a faint voice.

— My ex. How he used to take me. How he made me scream.

Daniel's body shuddered.

She continued slowly, saying things she had never dared to voice before:

— He would grip my hips… and enter me like the world was about to end. I still remember how my body responded. How I begged for more.

Daniel's fingers clenched the sheets. And then, like a switch had flipped, something happened.

He hardened.

Not just from anger or jealousy but pure desire. His body responded.

And she felt it—under her fingers, beneath her belly—a real erection. Almost feral.

What followed was something they had never experienced before. There was no sweet love, no caution.

There was urgency. Hunger. Release.

Isadora rode him as if she were riding her own past, blending pain and pleasure, opening herself completely.

Daniel pulled her forcefully, eyes wide, overtaken by a desire that seemed to come from a place the illness couldn't touch.

They made love as if meeting for the first time. As if the abyss between them had, for one night, ceased to exist.

Afterwards, lying side by side, sweaty and breathless, Daniel murmured:

— I never thought hearing that… could wake something in me. But it was real. You woke me up, Isa.

She didn't answer. Because inside her, there were still questions without names.

But in that moment, on that bed, she knew one thing for sure:

Desire is a strange animal.

And sometimes, to reignite it, you must also light the shadows.

The next morning, sunlight slipped through the curtain like a silent sign that the world hadn't stopped—though for Isadora, something had changed irreversibly.

Daniel was still asleep, arms relaxed and breathing heavy. He looked at peace. Relieved.

She watched him for a few seconds, trying to decipher what she felt.

The previous night still pulsed on her skin like a warm echo. It had been intense. Real.

But had it truly been her who was there?

Or just a version shaped by someone else's desires—a reflection created to reignite what had gone out?

She got up quietly. Passed through the living room, grabbed her phone, and went to the kitchen, where sunlight touched the old, tiled floor. She made coffee as if looking for answers in the routine.

As the aroma filled the room, Isadora leaned against the sink and thought.

Daniel's reaction had been real. So, had the desire.

But what about hers?

During the act, she had felt alive—yes. But also pierced by a question:

Had she achieved that connection only by invoking another man?

Had she truly surrendered to Daniel… or to the idea of being desired, of provoking, of having control over her own body?

The truth poked at her like a splinter under the skin: the experience had aroused her—but not just because of physical pleasure.

It was the power.

The dominance.

The freedom to transgress, even within the limits of a broken marriage.

When Daniel woke up later, with a shy smile and hopeful eyes, she smiled back—

but deep down, she knew this wasn't the end of the story.

It was the beginning of a new phase.

A phase where she would no longer live on autopilot.

A phase where, maybe for the first time, she could explore not just his desires… but her own.

And there, in front of the window, with the mug in her hands, Isadora whispered to herself:

— Life is calling me. And I won't pretend I don't hear it.

CHAPTER 6
THE FEAR OF THOSE WHO LOVE

Daniel woke up with a light body but a heavy soul.

The night before still throbbed in his mind like a memory too hot to ignore.

He had made love to Isadora like never before—not despite the illness, but because of it.

As if, by touching the edge of the abyss, he had discovered a new way to feel.

But with the euphoria came doubt.

He sat on the edge of the bed, feet on the cold floor, and stayed there for a few minutes.

He heard the kettle whistling in the kitchen, soft footsteps, and the breathing of their son in the next room.

And then he felt it: fear.

What had happened between them wasn't just sex. It was a rupture. A portal opening.

What if Isadora had liked that role too much?

What if that whisper—about another man, about a pleasure once lived—had been more than just provocation?

What if she had finally realized she no longer needed him—not as a husband, not as a lover, not even as a shadow of what they once were?

He got up slowly, splashed water on his face, and walked to the kitchen.

She was facing away, drinking coffee.

Calm. Serene. Almost distant.

— Did you sleep well? — he asked, with a shy smile.

She turned her face and nodded. But her eyes… were far away.

Daniel stepped closer, his hand lightly touching her hip.

— What happened last night… it was real to me. Very real. — He paused, searching for the right words. — But it was also scary.

She looked at him gently but without the same intensity of the night before.

— I know, Daniel.

— And you? How did you feel?

Isadora hesitated. She thought about lying, about saying what he needed to hear.

But something inside her wouldn't let her.

— Free — she answered, without disguise. — For the first time in a long time.

Daniel felt the ground shift beneath his feet.

It was what he most wanted to hear… and, at the same time, what he most feared.

Because love, he realized, isn't always about holding on.

Sometimes, it's about letting go.

And in that moment, in the middle of that sunlit kitchen, Daniel understood:

If he truly wanted to keep Isadora close, he would have to accept that she was changing.

And that perhaps the truest kind of love is the one that survives even when the roles are no longer the same.

In the days that followed, Daniel watched Isadora blossom.

It was subtle but clear—in the way she got dressed in the morning, in the lightness with which she moved around the house, in the spark that was slowly returning to her eyes.

She was being reborn.

And he, standing at the edge of the path, tried to figure out what to do with this rebirth that didn't fully include him.

She never mentioned the ménage again.

Didn't bring up another man nor resumed the provocative whispers from that night when his body had responded in a way it hadn't in months.

But Daniel knew it wasn't buried.

It was just paused. Growing.

Like a seed about to break through the earth.

One afternoon, he found a browser tab left open on the computer—

A discreet forum for open-minded couples.

Anonymous profiles. Stories. People looking for connections with consent, with clear rules.

Daniel closed the tab without touching anything.

And for the first time, felt something stronger than fear: jealousy mixed with arousal.

It was strange thinking of her with another man hurt…

But it also made him feel alive again.

As if, in some twisted way, his own desire depended on her freedom.

That night, while they were washing the dishes, he broke the silence:

— Are you thinking of going through with it?

Isadora didn't pretend.

She dried her hands, turned to face him, and answered calmly:

— I'm thinking about me. About whom I was before I became just a mother, just a wife, just a survivor.

Daniel took a deep breath.

He knew she wasn't saying it to be cruel.

She was just being honest.

Something rare between couples used to pretending they're still the same.

— And where do I fit into all this? — he asked, not in a demanding tone, but like someone trying to understand his place on a new map.

Isadora stepped closer. She placed her hand gently on his face.

— You fit… if you want to. But in a unique way than we imagined.

I don't want to leave you, Daniel. I just can't abandon myself for anyone anymore. Not even for love.

He nodded. And in that moment, he understood something simple and brutal:

To absolutely love someone, sometimes you must relearn how to love without owning.

Daniel had spent the night awake, listening to her breathing beside him. There was a silence between them that wasn't empty anymore— but too full. As if every unspoken word, every undone gesture, was building a new language between them—a language where love and fear walked hand in hand, like old companions. He wanted to touch her but wasn't sure if it was out of desire, out of attachment, or just to make sure she was still there.

Isadora, on the other hand, felt a strange kind of peace. She had cried alone in the bathroom that morning—not from sadness, but from something new and nameless. It was like mourning a version of herself she no longer recognized. When she saw Daniel in the hallway, eyes hollow and soul stripped bare, she felt tenderness. But she also felt pity. And that hurt more than she expected.

That afternoon, she took a bus into the city alone—just to walk among strangers. She sat on a park bench and watched life move as if watching an old film. She thought of Daniel. Of how he had been her anchor for so long and how now she wanted to fly—not away from him, but out of herself. She wondered if it was possible to still love someone and yet walk a different path. She wondered if he could walk beside her without pulling her back.

Daniel, meanwhile, had started writing. Fragments. Loose thoughts. It wasn't a diary nor poetry—just words, like a mirror in which he tried to find himself again. He wrote that he loved her. He wrote that he felt angry. He wrote that he was lost. And, for the first time, he admitted he might be jealous of her courage. Because deep down, he also wanted to become someone else—but didn't know where to begin.

On a rainy Sunday, they were stuck at home, sitting on the couch in silence. Their son slept in the next room. Isadora picked up a book. Daniel picked up nothing. He just watched her. And then, in a voice barely above a whisper, like a child's, he asked:

— Do you still love me?

She closed the book gently. Looked at him, long and searching, as if trying to find the answer inside him—not inside herself.

— I do. But maybe not in the same way.

He nodded. He didn't protest. He just felt a deep, familiar ache in his chest—not because he was losing Isadora, but because he was losing who he had been with her.

That night, when she held him in bed, it was Daniel who cried first. His body trembled in her arms, and she simply held him tighter. She said nothing. Because sometimes, the cruellest thing is not the end of love—it's its rebirth in a form we haven't yet learned to understand.

CHAPTER 7
THE FIRST DOOR

That Friday night, Isadora left the house unhurried.

She dressed in care but without exaggeration.

Black pants, a loose, light silk blouse, her hair tied up in a way that revealed her neck.

Nothing flashy. Nothing vulgar.

But something about her sparkled — not in her clothes, but in her eyes.

Daniel stayed home with their son.

He didn't ask who she was meeting. He didn't want to know the details.

But his eyes followed her to the door with a mix of pride and pain.

Pride in seeing that woman becoming whole again.

And the pain in not knowing if she would ever come back to him the same.

The place was discreet — a small jazz bar tucked away in a downtown alley.

She had been messaging Leonardo for two weeks — a polite man, older, divorced, father to a girl the same age as her son.

They had talked about music, films, quiet fears, and the struggle of remaining someone beyond being a parent.

When he arrived, he wore a dark shirt and an old watch on his left wrist.

His eyes were calm, and his smile didn't try to impress. And because of that, it did.

They talked for hours. Nothing happened beyond the exchange of words.

But in that first meeting, Isadora realized something:

The freedom she sought wasn't about having every man in the world…

It was about being herself in front of any man.

When she got home, her son was already asleep.

Daniel was on the couch reading, though really he was just waiting.

"How was it?" he asked, without irony.

She sat beside him on the couch, took off her shoes, and rested her head on his shoulder, like she used to years ago.

"I just talked to someone. It was good."

He nodded in silence.

"And you? How did you feel?" she asked.

Daniel thought for a moment, then answered:

"Like I lost a part of you… but maybe I'm gaining another. A part I never knew. That maybe you didn't even know yourself."

She smiled, sad and beautiful.

"I'm just getting to know her now."

And there, in that dimly lit room, two bodies still side by side, trying to figure out if love could survive when it changed shape.

In the days following Isadora's meeting with Leonardo, Daniel lived a silent conflict.

Outwardly, he was the same — he took care of their son, worked, and shared the chores.

But inside, something trembled.

There were moments when he felt a strange, almost freeing pride in seeing her happy.

And others when jealousy crept in like an old animal, whispering that he was being left behind.

One night, he got up to get a glass of water.

Passing through the living room, he saw Isadora on the sofa, alone, on her phone.

She smiled when she saw him. He didn't smile back.

"Was it him?" he asked, straight.

She didn't lie:

"Yes."

Daniel sat down in front of her, still holding the glass.

"And when you're actually with him? When you sleep together?

What will I be to you after that?"

Isadora took her time to answer — not from hesitation, but because she was searching for a truth that wouldn't wound.

"I don't have that answer right now, Daniel. But I do know I don't want to live a lie just to preserve the image of a marriage."

He lowered his eyes.

It hurt, but it didn't surprise him.

They had long been living like tired siblings.

Sex had been a flicker.

Life together, a series of attempts.

"Do you know what scares me most?" he murmured.

"Losing you… even while you're still here."

She touched his hand.

"In some ways, you already have. But that doesn't mean it's over.

It's just… changed."

Daniel took a deep breath.

He knew there was a world of difference between 'losing' and 'letting go'.

And maybe he still had the power to choose how to live within this new logic.

"I'm willing to try," he said, finally.

"But I need to know I still matter.

That there's still room for me, even if another man enters your life."

Isadora smiled gently.

She stood, sat on his lap, and held him like it was their last chance.

"You're part of my story, Daniel.

I just don't know if you're still the main character.

But that… we can find out together. Or not."

And there, in the silence of that night,

a man learned that loving sometimes means staying when everything says to leave.

And a woman learned that leaving isn't always running away — sometimes, it's returning to herself.

The next night, Isadora came home later.

Daniel was already in bed but still awake.

The room was dark. The lamp was off.

She came in quietly and undressed slowly.

It wasn't a striptease — it was an intimate gesture like she was removing more than fabric: guilt, doubt, exhaustion.

In the dark, he smelled her — her perfume mixed with something new. Maybe the street. Maybe a memory.

She lay down beside him.

Said nothing.

Just touched him lightly, her fingers on his shoulders.

Daniel, tense, didn't move at first.

But her touch was warm, sincere.

And his body, despite the wounded pride, still wanted her — maybe more than ever.

When they turned to face each other, there were no certainties.

Only hunger.

Isadora pressed her lips to his with a sweetness that burned.

It wasn't possession. It was surrender.

And Daniel responded.

First, slowly, like testing unfamiliar ground.

Then, with an urgency he didn't know he still had.

She climbed onto him, legs strong, firm, assured.

But her eyes… her eyes were full of tears.

Not sadness — intensity.

Like someone feeling everything at once.

Daniel ran his hands down her back and gripped her tight as if trying to hold onto time, the moment, whatever was still between them.

The sex was more than physical.

It was sweaty, slow, dense.

It held rage, longing, jealousy, and love.

Isadora moaned softly, eyes closed, as if diving deep into herself.

Daniel shifted between raw pleasure and an almost reverent gaze — as if watching a woman being reborn before him… and still his.

When they finished, they said nothing.

She lay on her side, back to him.

And after a few seconds, he held her from behind.

His body still pulsed, but now it was silence that hurt.

Because they had crossed another door.

And neither knew what lay beyond.

"Were you thinking about him?" Daniel asked his mouth against the back of her neck.

Isadora closed her eyes. Answered without turning:

"No. Just me. And you. Together."

He nodded, swallowing the bitter taste of doubt.

But deep down, it brought him peace.

Because maybe, just maybe, he was still part of her new desire — even if in a different form.

She turned to him and touched his face.

"I don't know if I can promise fidelity with my body. But I can promise presence. Honesty. And desire… if you still want me."

Daniel took a deep breath.

Her scent, her sweaty skin, her open gaze — everything was hers.

But everything was different.

"I do. But I need to learn how to want you your way."

She smiled, eyes full of devastating tenderness.

"Then we'll learn together. Through mistakes, through touch, through surprise."

That night, they made love again.

Not with fury, but with slow hunger.

As if reading an old book aloud, page by page.

And for the first time, Daniel understood that maybe love is this:

Not clinging to what once was but desiring what is being born — even if it frightens.

Even if it hurts.

Even if it doesn't yet have a name.

The cold was the first to arrive every morning. Not the cold of winter — that she had already learned to face with borrowed coats and strong coffee. It was another cold, deeper, coming from inside, even with a warm body beside her.

They had been married for almost twelve years. They lived in a small apartment, smelling of fried food stuck to the walls and neighbours speaking loudly in a language Isadora still stumbled to understand.

Daniel left early for the construction site. He returned dirty with cement and silence. He was a good man — hardworking, honest, dedicated. But he wasn't always present. And, little by little, Isadora began to realize that physical presence wasn't enough.

At night, lying beside him, she felt the old loneliness slowly returning. The one that had lived inside her since she was a girl. Since her father disappeared from the world without ever saying, "I'm leaving." Since her mother became absent. Since her grandmother, with her prayers and rules, tried to fill her with faith that only love could heal.

Isadora had grown up without long embraces, without someone to protect her when fear knocked. She carried childhood like a poorly healed scar. And that was why, even now, married, in a new country, she still sought something she didn't quite know how to name.

It wasn't just love. It was belonging. It was the desire to finally be someone's priority.

Daniel was everything she had ever dreamed of — and everything she still lacked.

Because Isadora didn't want just a home, food, or a shared bed.

She wanted to be seen. She wanted him to see what she couldn't even explain:

The needy girl, raised with difficulty, taught to be silent and obedient.

The woman who still thought she had to earn love — as if love were a prize.

She never said this to him. She stayed quiet. Played her roles — wife, immigrant, warrior.

But sometimes, in the middle of the night, she cried softly, face turned to the wall.

Daniel slept deeply. And she, too light, almost transparent from so much self-denial.

He said they were building a life. That it was just a matter of time before everything would settle, and it was true. But there was a part of Isadora that couldn't wait anymore.

It wasn't impatience. It was exhaustion. Exhaustion from being strong, from swallowing tears, from being the woman who "holds on." Exhaustion from pretending it didn't hurt to be alone even inside the house.

She did everything: cooked, cleaned, saved money. And at the end of the day, she waited. Waited for a gesture, a listening, a tenderness that wasn't just now of touch. Waited to be noticed without asking. But Daniel was practical. The type who solved with actions what she needed in words.

When she tried to open, he said it was a phase, that soon everything would get better. And she smiled, nodded, swallowed again the urge to scream: "But what about me? Who takes care of me?"

During video calls with her grandmother, she pretended to be happy. The old woman, now slower, more fragile, still said the same things: "A woman must be strong. Hang in there, my daughter. Marriage is like that."

And Isadora hung up with a tighter chest than before.

She started writing in a hidden notebook. Loose things. Confused feelings.

Sometimes just a phrase: "Today I felt invisible." "Today, I remembered the girl who dreamed of being loved." "Today, I thought about leaving."

She didn't really want to leave. Not yet. But for the first time, she considered that she deserved something different. Not better — different. Something lighter, more honest, more whole.

And in that silence between what she lived and what she dreamed, Isadora began to wake up. Not from a nightmare. But from the role that had been written for her before she even had a chance to choose.

A few days later, Daniel came home later than usual. His face was tense, his shoulders more slumped than normal. He tossed his backpack in the corner and opened the fridge silently.

"Is everything okay?" she asked, trying to sound casual.

He hesitated before answering.

"They let half the team go today." He took a deep breath. "I think I'm next."

Isadora felt the ground give a slight jolt. Not because of the risk of losing his job — but because, for a moment, he seemed vulnerable. Human. Fragile.

She thought about saying that she also felt lost, alone, tired. Thought about telling him about the hidden notebooks, the nights spent crying silently, the fear of disappearing inside a role she never chose.

She even thought about saying, "I'm not happy, Daniel."

But she didn't say it.

Instead, she got up slowly, took a plate with rice and meat she had reserved for him, and put it in the microwave.

The usual gesture.

The usual routine.

He ate in silence, staring at the television tuned to a program neither of them really followed.

And it was there, in that warm, domestic scene, that Isadora knew:

She wasn't going to leave.

Not now.

Not yet.

Not because everything was fine.

But because it was what she knew.

Because leaving needed a strength she didn't have yet.

Because the fear of starting over alone was still greater than the pain of staying.

Later, she lay down beside him, who was already asleep.

She stared at the ceiling for a long time, her hand resting on her empty belly, her heart pounding with silence.

Tomorrow, she would make coffee early.

Wash the clothes.

Call her grandmother.

And she would say — as she always said — that everything was all right.

Even when inside, everything still screamed.

The next morning, Isadora awoke before the alarm. The sky was cloaked in darkness, and the house lay wrapped in a familiar silence. She rose slowly, careful not to wake Daniel. Water warmed on the stove; coffee grounds measured with quiet reverence. She moved through the tiny kitchen like one performing a sacred ritual—not from faith, but from sheer survival.

As the rich aroma filled the air, she watched herself as if from afar—another woman moving on autopilot. She saw her cracked fingers from endless dishwashing, the shadows beneath her eyes no concealer could hide. She thought how no one truly saw her like this: whole, weary, relentless.

She opened the window and let the chilly wind brush her face. For a fleeting moment, tears threatened to fall—but she held them back. Nighttime was the keeper of her sorrow.

Daniel appeared from the bedroom with heavy steps, eyes still half-shut. She poured the coffee as always. He nodded in thanks, wordless. They sat across the table, separated by an invisible gulf.

"Did you sleep well?" she ventured softly.

"More or less," he replied, never asking in return.

She nodded. That was enough. She'd learned expecting reciprocity was like planting flowers in concrete.

After he left, she retrieved the hidden notebook from the back of the drawer. With small, hesitant script, she wrote:

"Today, I thought perhaps I must find myself before waiting to be found."

Closing the notebook, she tucked it away like a precious secret. She donned her coat, grabbed her cloth bag, and stepped out to the market. On the way, she met Mrs. Zulema, her neighbour from 301, who offered a warm smile and slow words in a blend of Portuguese and Spanish.

"How are you, Isadora?"

She hesitated, tempted to share the truth. Instead, she smiled.

"I'm fine, yes. And you?"

They exchanged polite words, but inside, something stirred—a fragile thread of strength beginning to grow. Not yet courage, but awareness. And she knew awareness was the first breath of change.

At the market, she paused before the vibrant shelves of fruit and remembered her childhood days at the market with her grandmother. Mangoes plucked and sucked straight from the tree, laughter spilling freely, untouched by judgment. She recalled the lightness she once carried. She could carry it again.

On her way home, she stopped before a cosmetics store window. There, in the mirror, she saw herself whole—hair carelessly tied, worn clothes—but most of all, she saw her eyes. Still shining. Faintly but unmistakably shining.

And she promised herself, without voice, without drama:

"One day, I will choose myself. Even if only for a moment."

Arriving home, she put away the groceries, cleaned the floor, and organized the closet.

And by late afternoon, she sat alone on the balcony, a cup of hot tea warming her hands.

The world outside kept its usual rhythm—honking cars, hurried footsteps, children shouting in the courtyard.

But inside her, something was beginning to change.

It was not a revolution. It was a seed.

CHAPTER 9
WHAT HE ALSO DOESN'T SAY

Daniel never quite knew how to handle words.

He learned early that a real man speaks little, works hard, and doesn't complain.

He grew up hearing his father say, "Feelings are things you sort out in silence."

And that's how he became who he was: through effort, sweat, a tired body, and a tight chest he couldn't even name.

When he married Isadora, he believed he could manage it.

That working hard, paying the bills, putting food on the table was enough.

That was love, wasn't it? Being present. Providing the basics. Being faithful. Never raising his voice.

But over time, he noticed a space between them, a gap that even the furniture couldn't hide.

Isadora smiled less. Spoke less. Sometimes, the way she looked at him seemed distant—

As if she expected something he didn't know how to give.

And it hurt. Deeply.

But he didn't say it.

Not for lack of wanting—but lack of knowing how.

Because even though he wanted to, he didn't know how to ask:

"What do you need from me beyond what I already give?"

And worse—he wasn't sure if he'd want the answer.

He worked construction before the sun rose.

Managed concrete, dirt, the weight of carrying a whole life on his back.

And now, with company cuts, the shadow of losing his job haunted him.

Uncertainty was a ghost he couldn't escape.

He felt small. Useless. A burden.

That night, when he came home late, his shoulders ached, but his soul weighed heavier.

When Isadora asked if he was all right, for a moment he wanted to say everything.

To tell her he was scared. That he felt himself losing her without knowing why.

Sometimes he cried in the bathroom, under the shower, so no one would hear.

But he swallowed it all.

He only said, "I think I'm next."

And waited for her to explode, to ask what they'd do, to panic, to blame him.

But she just got up and put his plate in the microwave.

That simple gesture broke him inside.

Yes, routine—but at that moment, he saw care there.

He saw her effort to keep going.

And deep down, he felt ashamed.

Because he knew she deserved more.

More than half a man who lived trying to be whole through practical acts alone.

That night, he slept lighter—not because things were all right, but because he let himself fall a little.

Show a crack.

And, strange as it seemed, he felt less alone.

In the days that followed, he began to watch her more closely.

The silences. The lowered eyes.

The way she absentmindedly touched her belly, as if caressing an absence.

He thought about asking:

"Are you still happy with me?"

"Do you dream of another life?"

But he didn't.

Because he was afraid of the answer.

And because he still believed if he woke early, didn't miss work, took out the rubbish, and put food on the table, everything would be fine.

That's what his father said.

That's what men learn to repeat.

But now, Daniel was starting to doubt.

Because for the first time, he felt he might be losing the woman he loved most—not to betrayal, fight, or abandonment,

But because he couldn't see her properly.

And that, he knew, was a cruel kind of abandonment, too.

The following week, Daniel woke every day with a thought pounding like a jackhammer:

"What if I'm the one who holds her back?

What if my love is what stops her from being happy?"

It wasn't drama. It was realization.

And the more he looked at Isadora, the more he saw how much she shrank inside.

Her lightness had become effort.

Her smile, a rarity.

Her touch, a habit—not desire.

He remembered the woman he met—strong, laughing, full of plans.

And now, he saw a shadow.

A woman on autopilot.

Who cared for everything but walked with distant eyes.

Like someone always on the verge of leaving but without direction.

Daniel wasn't dumb. Nor blind.

He knew he wasn't cheating, but he also knew he was failing somehow.

And then, on a rainy Sunday afternoon, sitting alone on the balcony with a warm beer in hand, he thought something he never had before:

"If she's not happy with me, shouldn't I let her go?"

He swallowed hard.

Tasted not just the bitter drink but the bitter thought.

Because he loved her.

In his own way—yes, crooked, restrained, silent.

But he loved her.

Only love, he was beginning to understand, might not be about holding on.

It was also about knowing how to let go.

That night, he didn't sleep.

He tossed and turned in bed, listening to Isadora's steady breathing beside him.

He thought of everything they had lived together:

The simple wedding, the move to another country, the bills paid with sacrifice, Sundays on the couch with movies, nights spent holding each other without saying a word.

It wasn't little.

But it wasn't everything either.

And for the first time, Daniel admitted to himself that it wasn't enough for her.

Maybe Isadora needed something more than he could give.

Not out of cruelty. Not out of neglect.

But because he didn't know how to be that "more."

And then he decided.

The next day, when she came back from the market and took off her shoes at the door,

he called to her.

"Isadora... can I say something?"

She stopped, looking at him with a mix of surprise and caution.

"Sure. What is it?"

He took a deep breath. His voice was softer than he intended but steady:

"If one day... if you think you need to go... or to live something else... or be with someone who sees you the way I can't... you can. Okay?"

She frowned, not understanding at first.

"What do you mean?"

He swallowed hard.

"I love you. So much. But I'm starting to understand that... love is also wanting to see the other happy. Even if it's not with us."

She was silent, the bag still in her hands, frozen in the kitchen doorway.

Daniel kept his eyes on the floor:

"I'm not saying I want you to leave. Or that I want us to end.

I'm just saying that if one day you feel you need something different...

I won't hold you back.

You deserve to feel alive again. Whole. Loved the way you dream."

When he looked up, she was still there, motionless.

No tears. No words.

Just that thick, old silence, full of everything they never managed to say to each other.

And it was in that silence that he felt—for the first time—that he had done something right.

Not as a practical man, provider, or worker.

But as a human being.

That night, they lay down in silence.

But something between them had changed.

It wasn't a break.

It was freedom.

It hurt.

But it set them free.

CHAPTER 10
FIRST STEPS: ABYSS OR PARADISE?

It was strange at first. Strange and frightening.

But also freeing.

The conversation between them had happened a few days earlier.

Sitting at the kitchen table, no fights, no tears—just two people finally trying to be honest.

Daniel, eyes lowered, said he no longer wanted to be the limit of Isadora's happiness.

She, with teary eyes, confessed she no longer knew where the woman she truly was ended and the one she pretended to be began.

Together, they decided they would make space.

Space for desire, for rediscovery, for a kind of freedom that didn't feel like betrayal but rescue.

The initiative came from him.

The permission too.

Not as someone giving in but as someone who loves enough to accept that the other needs more.

On Friday night, Daniel brought the laptop from the living room to the bedroom.

They placed it on the still-unmade bed and sat side by side like two nervous teenagers about to do something forbidden.

"Are you sure?" she asked for the third time.

He nodded, trying to smile.

"I just want you to feel alive. This doesn't change what we are."

Isadora took a deep breath.

She created a profile on a discreet dating site.

No real name, no explicit photos.

Just words—honest, heavy with had desire and an old hunger to be seen, desired, discovered.

In the "About Me" section, she wrote:

"Mature woman, curious, looking to reconnect with my own body and the pleasure that had fallen asleep.

I'm in an open and respectful relationship. I want to feel again. I want to be chosen without having to deserve it."

Daniel read over her shoulder.

He said nothing. But inside, a knot formed.

Not jealousy.

But mourning.

Because even though he supported her, he knew something would die there.

A part of the idealized romantic love.

The idea of exclusivity.

The man who thought being good and present was enough.

But something new was also born.

Respect. Courage. Truth.

In the following days, she received messages.

Some vulgar, others sincere.

One or two men caught her attention.

One especially: Gabriel.

38 years old, divorced, literature professor.

They exchanged long messages at night while Daniel washed the dishes in the kitchen with headphones on.

She laughed quietly, like someone remembering how to laugh like that.

On Wednesday, she showed the conversation to Daniel.

"He seems respectful," she said as if asking for permission.

He just nodded silently. His heart tightened.

But he stayed.

Stayed because that was the choice.

And because, despite the pain, it was still love.

On Friday, she went out on the date.

She dressed up like she hadn't in years.

Red lipstick.

New perfume.

A sparkle in her eyes he recognized with surprise—

the sparkle of someone about to find themselves again.

When she closed the door behind her, Daniel stood still, staring at the silence of the house.

And for the first time, he understood that sometimes the greatest act of love is not to fight to hold on.

It's to open the door.

And wait for the other to come back—not because they have to.

But because they want to.

As the day of the date approached, something different began to grow between them.

It wasn't distance—quite the opposite.

It was as if suddenly they were more alive, more aware, more electric.

As if the abyss that had opened before them forced them to look at each other with honesty that hadn't existed in years.

On Monday, after dinner, Isadora took off her shirt in front of him without saying a word.

Not to provoke.

But because she no longer needed to hide the body, she was starting to recognize it as her own again.

Daniel stood there, watching.

Not as a husband used to the routine—but as a man, wanting a woman who suddenly seemed like someone else.

Or had always been that way, and he had just stopped seeing.

That night, they made love like they hadn't in a long time.

With fury.

With fear.

With tenderness and brutality mixed.

She was intense.

He was hungry.

As Daniel kissed her, his heart tightened—not just from love or jealousy, but from vertigo.

Because this—her body surrendered, her pleasure free—now came with another layer:

The thought that soon, maybe, she would be like this with someone else.

And just thinking about it, something inside Daniel ignited.

Something primitive. Confused. Erotic. Painful.

Am I crazy? he wondered.

Am I a masochist for wanting this woman so much right now when she's starting to let go for the world?

But it was true.

His desire for Isadora grew with every message she exchanged with that man.

With every muffled laugh, she gave, looking at her phone.

With every time, she said:

— I'm going to take a shower… be right back.

Her scent, the sound of her breathing, the way she walked around the house lightly, with a sparkle in her eyes he hadn't seen in ages—all of it pushed Daniel to the edge.

By day, he worked with cement and concrete.

By night, he lived in a raw state of desire.

And the strangest part: it wasn't about sex.

It was about seeing her alive.

About wanting the woman who was finally wanting herself.

They started making love more often, more intensely.

On Wednesday, on the sofa.

On Thursday, leaning against the bathroom wall.

On Friday morning, before she left, he pulled her by the waist and made love like someone who knows it might be the last time like that—just the two of them.

And Isadora, for the first time, let herself orgasm without guilt.

Without fear of seeming too much.

Because now she knew: Daniel saw her.

Even if, for that, she had to almost leave him.

In Daniel's mind, the image of her with another man was unbearable.

And at the same time, fascinating.

Not from perversion.

But because deep down, he wanted to see Isadora whole.

Even if it was through another's eyes.

And that contradiction drove him crazy.

With desire.

With doubt.

With love.

The next night, when she returned from her second date with Gabriel, Daniel was still awake. Sitting in the armchair, dim light casting shadows, a full glass of wine trembling in his hands. She entered quietly, slipping off her shoes, her face flushed—not with shame, but with heat. With life. With desire freshly awakened.

He looked at her for a few seconds. He wanted to ask everything but couldn't. The silence between them was thick, almost liquid. She walked over, perched on the arm of the chair, and pressed her lips softly to his forehead. A simple gesture, yet heavy with confession. He smelled another man's scent on her skin—and did not pull away.

"Do you want to know?" she whispered.

Daniel lifted his eyes. There was pain there but no accusation. He nodded slowly, like someone accepting something irreversible.

"It was intense," she said. "But it wasn't about him. It was about me. About my body, remembering it still exists. About my skin responding. About coming without having to ask permission."

Daniel closed his eyes for a moment, trying to breathe through the avalanche. The image of Isadora with another man struck him like lightning. It burned. But strangely, it also ignited him inside. His body reacted before his mind. Jealousy came with the erection. Fear with hunger.

She slid from the chair into his lap. Legs wrapped around his waist, mouth close to his ear.

"And now? Do you still want me?" she teased cruelly.

But Daniel was already hard. Already lost in her again.

"More than ever," he answered with sweet rage, biting her neck.

Right there in the living room, curtains still open to the night, they made love like forbidden lovers. Like everything could end any second, she rode him, setting the pace. Eyes locked on his. There was no romance. There was lust. There was territory. She marked his skin with her nails. He gripped her thighs, trying not to shatter.

When she came, she bit his shoulder hard. When he came, he cried. Quietly. Without noise. Like someone who understands something has broken and will never be the same, but, at the same time, something new was born there—wild, fragile, and bright like fire in the wind.

Lying naked and breathless afterwards, Isadora traced her fingers across his chest.

"It's still you, Daniel. It's still with you that I come back."

He said nothing. He just held her hand. And in that touch, there was everything: anger, desire, fear, love.

And a silent promise: if we're to fall into this abyss, let's do it hand in hand.

Chapter 11
Fourteen Hours

Hour 1 — The Fire

The touch was the first flame.

Gabriel was in no hurry.

He held her by the waist like something sacred—and at the same time wild.

The kiss was deeper than she remembered it could be.

It wasn't just lips—it was the whole body opening up, skin tingling even before being touched.

When he pressed her against the living room wall, the dress rose with the ease of someone who knew exactly what they were doing.

Isadora arched her body.

Eyes closed.

Breath ragged.

Gabriel explored her like reading an ancient map.

Without fear of getting lost.

And there, on the cold floor, in the urgency of their bodies, she had her first orgasm—intense, overwhelming, made of moans held back for years.

Daniel had never seen her like that.

Hour 2 — The Laughter

Later, still lying down, she laughed.

A light, almost childish laugh.

One of those that comes when the soul finally exhales the air it has been holding for a long time.

Gabriel looked at her like one contemplates a rare sunset.

— What is it? — he asked, voice husky.

— I felt alive — she answered.

The second hour was filled with slower, sweeter touches.

Tongue sliding reverently.

Fingers mapping every inch as if wanting to memorize it.

She let herself ask, guide, say what she liked.

And he listened.

She had never been heard like that before.

Neither in bed nor outside of it.

The second orgasm came like a gentle wave.

Sneaky, steady.

And made her tremble all over.

Hour 3 — The Surrender

They went upstairs to the bedroom.

Isadora walked with feverish skin and eyes shining like in a trance.

The mirror reflected a woman she didn't recognize—or rather, one she had forgotten existed.

Gabriel laid her down on the bed slowly, and this time it was different.

There was no hurry anymore.

There was worship.

She opened herself—literally and symbolically.

Let him penetrate her with intensity, yes, but also with a look that said, "I see you."

There, in the deep, rhythmic coming and going, she cried.

Not from pain.

Nor sadness.

She cried because something inside her was unravelling.

Something ancient, rooted.

And came the third orgasm.

Long.

Slow.

Silent.

Hour 4 — The Final Gesture

In the last hour, he knelt before her.

Kissed her feet, her thighs, her belly.

And then went down.

Isadora surrendered and didn't hesitate. She closed her eyes and let the pleasure rise in waves.

One, two, three times.

And when he reached the limits of what he could offer with his mouth and desire, she felt something she hadn't felt in years: gratitude for her own body.

Gratitude for still being able to feel.

Gratitude for not having left herself behind.

Gabriel finished with a gesture of contemplation.

And she, exhausted, lying on the rumpled sheet, felt as if the world had stopped.

For four hours, it had been nothing but desire, sweat, and truth.

In the silence that followed, Isadora knew:

She would never be the same again.

She watched him there—surrendered, vulnerable, eyes closed as if in complete trust.

She felt an impulse that wasn't only physical but a mixture of curiosity, generosity, and power.

She wanted to give him what he had just given her—without haste, without shame, without limits.

She knelt slowly, keeping her eyes on his.

And touched him with reverence, like one touch of an ancient truth.

Her mouth, warm and steady, moved in its own rhythm—sometimes intense, sometimes gentle.

She was guided not by urgency but by the desire to see him break apart, just as she had broken before.

Gabriel arched his body.

He groaned softly.

Murmured her name as if praying.

And at the peak, when pleasure took over every inch of him, she stayed there.

Without looking away. Without hesitation.

At that moment, she was not just a woman.

She was whole.

She was free.

And when he fell beside her, breathless and smiling, Isadora looked at him with a new serenity.

It wasn't love—not yet.

But it was the beginning of something she had never experienced:

The feeling of being completely desired.

The farewell was silent but intense.

Gabriel looked at Isadora with a smile that mixed complicity and admiration.

He touched her gently as if not wanting to let the beauty of the moment slip away.

She, still lying on the bed, her skin glowing as if the sun had poured over her, looked at him with a gaze that said it all: gratitude, desire, and something more—something deeper that she was still trying to understand.

He didn't ask anything because, at some point, he also knew words weren't necessary.

They kissed. Slow. Long.

It was a goodbye kiss but also one of recognition.

Of a moment lived.

Of a new woman rising inside her—stronger, more confident, more... free.

When Gabriel got up and left, Isadora stayed there in the dimness of the room.

Silence took over the space, but inside her, everything was boiling.

She sat on the bed and picked up her phone, still with her hands trembling a little.

She had recorded it.

That intimate encounter.

Images of a woman she had never imagined herself to be.

Videos that captured the intensity of it all—the sensuality, the freedom, the surrender.

The Isadora she didn't know but now felt.

The woman driven by her own strength, by her own freedom.

She watched the videos, a smile on her lips—a satisfied smile.

Her skin gleamed with pleasure, discovery, a kind of power she had finally learned to have.

She was no longer the silent wife, the invisible woman.

She was Isadora in her purest essence.

A woman who understood that pleasure wasn't just a right—it was an affirmation of her existence.

A soft laugh arose, and the smile stayed.

She no longer felt lost. Nor guilty.

She felt radiant.

Free.

There, in that moment, with the phone in her hand, she understood something she had never understood before:

Pleasure was hers, not someone else's.

And she no longer cared about others' expectations.

Isadora had been reborn.

And now, she knew she was ready to live her own story.

The room was still heavy with the scent of their passion, but inside Isadora, something far greater had ignited. It wasn't just the memory of touch or the echo of pleasure — it was a raw, awakening fire that had lain dormant beneath years of silence and restraint. She ran her hands over her skin, marvelling at the woman she saw in the mirror — fierce, radiant, and utterly unbound.

Gabriel's presence lingered like a ghost, but not one that haunted her. Instead, it whispered of freedom, of desires claimed and no longer hidden. Her lips curled into a smile, sharp and knowing. For the first time, she understood that her pleasure wasn't a secret sin but a rebellion, a reclaiming of power long stolen by fear and expectation.

Her phone buzzed quietly in the dim light, pulling her back to the fragile threads of her other life. A message from Daniel blinked on the screen: "Thinking of you." Her heart tightened, a knot of longing and guilt weaving through her chest. But instead of shrinking away, she typed back simply, "Me too." No explanations, no apologies — just two souls holding onto each other amid the chaos of new truths.

The air between her and Daniel had shifted palpably. When he returned, she noticed the way his eyes lingered on her with a mix of awe and vulnerability. There was pain there, yes, but also something deeper — a willingness to accept the unknown, to love her not despite this change but because of it. They didn't need words; their hands entwined spoke the language of fragile hope.

Alone again, Isadora sat by the window and watched the city move beneath the darkening sky. She felt untethered but unafraid, as if the ground beneath her had shifted and revealed a new world waiting to be explored. The woman she had been, the one she was becoming — they coexisted in a delicate balance of past and possibility.

Memories of Gabriel's touch surged back — gentle yet commanding, reverent yet wild. She understood now that desire was not a chain but a key, unlocking parts of her she had long ignored. Her laughter, light and free, bubbled up unexpectedly. She was no longer hiding. She was found.

In the quiet of the night, Isadora made a silent vow to herself. She would no longer live behind walls of fear or silence. Her body, her desires, her essence were hers alone to honour. She was a woman reborn from the ashes of restraint, blazing with the fierce light of her own becoming.

Daniel's gaze met hers across the room one evening, and in that look, a thousand unspoken emotions passed — love, longing, pain, and acceptance. They were no longer just spouses; they were two souls learning how to love without cages, without limits, even if it meant stepping into the unknown together.

As the days passed, Isadora found herself moving with new grace, a woman reclaiming space she never knew she had lost. The freedom she tasted with Gabriel was no longer just a memory but a foundation — a reminder that she was worthy of being desired, seen, and loved in all her complexity.

And beneath it all, in the quiet depths of her heart, a fire burned steady and sure — a fire that promised she would never again settle for anything less than the truth of her own desire and the unshakable power of her own freedom.

CHAPTER 12
THE BEST NIGHT OF ALL

When Gabriel left, Isadora felt renewed, as if a weight had been lifted from her shoulders. She was radiant; her skin seemed to glow in a way she hadn't felt in years. It wasn't just physical pleasure; it was something deeper—a sense of freedom, of self-discovery. The woman she had become was there, stronger, more intense, more alive.

She picked up her phone and called Daniel. His voice, always familiar, came through the line.

"Hi, love. Are you coming home?" she asked with her usual calm.

"I'm there. How are you?" Daniel replied, noticing nothing different in her tone.

"All good, love. Everything's done here," Isadora said, with a smile, he couldn't see, but that shone through her voice.

She hung up the phone, still feeling the warmth of recent sensations flowing through her body. She looked at herself in the mirror, seeing herself in a way she never had before. The woman before her was more confident, surer, and free.

When Daniel arrived, he entered the house with the familiar scent of the street and work. But as he crossed the door, he felt something different. The air carried a mix of perfume and something else—something he couldn't name but at once recognized. It was the scent of another, something he didn't fully understand. He raised an eyebrow but said nothing.

Isadora was there, beautiful as always, but with a sparkle in her eyes he had never seen. She approached him, and before he could say anything, she enveloped him in a long, intense kiss. It was a kiss unlike any other. There was no rush, no tension of everyday life. It was a kiss of reunion, of transformation.

Daniel, surprised by the intensity of the gesture, hesitated for a moment but soon gave in. Somehow, he realized that this was making her happy. She was being herself. And, although something inside him felt uncomfortable, he couldn't deny the pleasure he saw in her eyes, in the touch of her hands, in the way she kissed him.

Their child was sleeping deeply, and the atmosphere now felt quieter, more intimate. Daniel sat on the sofa, and Isadora joined him. They were silent for a moment, but something was different in the air. The space between them was no longer marked by expectations and responsibilities. It was as if a new connection was appearing from within them.

Isadora looked at Daniel and, with a softer voice than he had ever heard, said:

"Daniel, I want to tell you something. I… I found myself. Now I know who I am, who I really am."

He watched her, trying to process her words, but didn't know what to say. It was as if he was seeing a new woman, a woman who no longer depended on his answers or validation. She was already whole.

He touched her, and something in that gesture, in that simple touch, changed the course of the night. They drew closer, and something that had been postponed for so long, something buried deep in their relationship, happened. It wasn't just sex. It was a reconnection of souls, a surrender without reservations.

Their night stretched on for hours. It wasn't only physical pleasure that united them, but a deeper complicity, an exchange of energies both were thirsty for. They gave themselves to each other in a way they never had before, rediscovering their bodies and emotions, breaking down the barriers of everyday life, allowing themselves to be vulnerable but also strong. It was the night of love they both had hoped for—but in a way they never imagined.

In the end, tired but satisfied, they lay down together. Isadora, her skin glowing, looked at Daniel and whispered:

"I am more than you imagine, Daniel. And today, you saw me."

He looked into her eyes, now clearer than ever, and smiled. It was the smile of someone finally beginning to understand, even without words. He kissed her forehead, gently touched her face, and cuddled up beside her.

The night was long, but now, finally, everything seemed right. They didn't need more words. Their best night of love had been built not only on the body but on the soul.

Isadora felt every touch from Daniel like a new melody, a symphony of sensations celebrating the woman she had become. Her fingers glided over his skin with both delicacy and a fierce hunger — as if every inch of his body were sacred ground to be cherished and explored with reverence.

She loved the way he looked at her now, differently. Not with the tired gaze of routine but with a sparkle reflecting genuine surprise and desire. It was as if he were discovering a new Isadora — a woman made of fire and tenderness, able to give and receive with equal intensity.

Daniel's hands caressed her face with the same tenderness as before but then slowly moved downward, exploring curves and uncovering new pleasures. Each sigh she gave was an invitation, and he allowed himself to answer, breaking the distance built by time and routine.

Isadora closed her eyes, soaking in the joy of being truly seen, desired, and loved in her fullness. The heat of his body against hers was an embrace saying: "You are mine, whole and free." There were no demands, only surrender — a dance they learned with every movement.

She could feel his breath quicken, his heartbeat synchronising with hers. It was more than sex; it was a communion of souls long waiting to happen. And each touch, each kiss, was a reaffirmation that they could still reinvent themselves together.

Daniel kissed her collarbone, his warm lips leaving a trail of fire. Isadora arched her back, asking for more, wanting the moment to last forever. And he gave her everything — patience, desire, tenderness — in perfect harmony.

Their pleasure was a conversation without words, where every breath and moan told stories only they could understand. Isadora felt alive, powerful, the owner of her body and happiness — and that made the pleasure even more intense.

When Daniel lifted her in his arms and carried her to the bedroom, Isadora felt an electric current run through her whole body. There, in the sanctuary of intimacy, they rediscovered each other — not just as lovers but as two beings with so much more to offer.

She lay down on the bed, eyes locked with his, and they both lost themselves in that moment of absolute connection. Every touch was measured, every kiss a promise. Isadora knew it wasn't about satisfying desire — it was about celebrating the life they shared.

Daniel found the perfect rhythm, respecting her limits and desires, learning to listen to her body, her silences, her unspoken wishes. Isadora, in turn, surrendered without fear, knowing she was safe, loved, and valued.

The orgasm that came — long and deep — was like an explosion of light that illuminated every dark corner of her soul. It wasn't just physical — it was a release, a triumph over all the years of pain, silence, and repression.

She held Daniel tightly as if the world could end right there and they would be ready. Their bodies fit perfectly, in a harmony that seemed written in the stars. It was the first time she felt such a profound, true connection.

After the climax, soft whispers, gentle kisses, and words spoken in the silence of their gaze followed. They communicated without speaking, sharing an intimacy that went beyond the flesh, entering the realm of the spirit.

Isadora touched Daniel as if he were the most precious thing in the world, and he returned her affection in equal measure. Entwined, they felt something inside them change forever.

The night moved on, bringing with it the feeling that a new phase was beginning for the couple. No longer prisoners of social expectations or their own insecurities, but two partners finally understanding the true meaning of desire and love.

Isadora felt his body shiver under her hands, fuelling her desire, pleasure, and power. She no longer wanted to hide her strength; she wanted to shout to the world that she owned her happiness.

The heat she radiated was contagious, and Daniel got lost in that fire burning inside her but also warming him deeply. Their complicity was palpable, and despite the scars, love shone brighter than ever.

She sighed, feeling her body vibrate with satisfaction and peace. The best night ever wasn't about the act — it was about mutual surrender, the recognition of the other as a complete being, capable of feeling, surrendering, and loving without fear.

Finally, lying side by side, Isadora hugged Daniel, feeling his chest rise and fall with his breath. They were tired, but their souls vibrated coordinated, celebrating the victory of having rediscovered the pleasure of being together.

She whispered near his ear, her voice still trembling with emotion: "Tonight was more than love. It was our redemption."

And Daniel answered with a smile, the certainty that this night would be the foundation for a new beginning where both would finally be free.

CHAPTER 13
THE SILENT PAINS

After that intense and liberating night, Isadora felt different. There was a renewed sparkle in her eyes, a confidence she had never known she had. For the first time in a long time, she felt whole—as a woman, as a wife, as a person. The weight of expectations and limitations she had carried for years seemed to have vanished, replaced by something lighter, something truly hers.

But, although she was radiant, something inside Daniel had begun to break.

He had tried to hide it or pretend he hadn't felt it, but the pain of jealousy consumed him. Seeing his wife so happy, so alive, stirred feelings in him that he no longer knew how to control. He didn't fully understand what was happening—he knew he was happy for her, but at the same time, his own insecurity and old frustrations came back with force. He had been the man who was always there, but she had found something he could no longer give. Something he didn't know how to offer.

In the days that followed, Daniel began to pull away emotionally, not sure what was happening to him. The sadness he felt came like a rising wave, and he tried to fight it, but the shadows of his jealousy, mixed with guilt for not being enough, suffocated him. Every time he saw Isadora with that radiant smile, something inside him broke, but he couldn't say anything. He didn't want her to see his vulnerability.

He tried to be the husband she expected, but his actions didn't match the feelings he still didn't know how to process. The nights, which used to be moments of pleasure and closeness, now became uncomfortable, and without words, he isolated himself in the silent pain that consumed him.

Isadora, for her part, noticed the change. She felt something was different. Daniel was no longer the same, and although she saw him trying to stay strong, she felt the growing distance between them. It wasn't just a matter of physical closeness. He was absent in a deeper way, and Isadora couldn't understand what was going on. The conversations that once seemed natural started to be interrupted, silence taking the place of their intimacy.

She tried to reach out to him, tried to touch on delicate subjects, but he always evaded, and the feeling that he was keeping something to himself grew stronger every day. Words no longer came easily, and she began to sense the tension in the air. What once seemed the height of happiness for her was now a space filled with insecurity and doubt.

It didn't take long for Isadora to start questioning whether she had made the right choice. In her mind, she knew she was searching for something she needed—something her relationship with Daniel no longer seemed able to provide. But at the same time, the thought that he was now suffering, that he couldn't understand what she had done, made doubt begin to take over her mind. She could no longer ignore the signs that something was breaking between them.

The nights became even more silent. She began to withdraw, closing herself off, no longer wanting to force something that seemed to have lost its meaning. The arguments were small but frequent. She felt that, somehow, she had hurt Daniel but didn't know how to go back.

The desire that once seemed to drive them now became a burden. She no longer wanted to keep playing the game of hiding feelings, of trying to find something that was no longer there. Conversations about what had happened that night, about what she felt and what she wanted, were left hanging as if a dense cloud had settled between them.

"Daniel, I don't know anymore…" Isadora finally said one of those nights when they lay together but distant in the same bed. Her words were heavy with regret. She felt the consequences of her choices were hitting their relationship in a way she didn't know how to fix.

He looked at her, tired eyes, and in his expression, there was a silent pain, an understanding that something was no longer right. He still loved her, but the weight of what was happening between them was becoming unbearable. He didn't know how to give her what she wanted, and that made him feel increasingly inadequate.

"I don't know anymore, Isadora. I don't know either," he replied in a deep voice, but full of a weight she knew was the reflection of his inner frustration.

It was there, that silent night, that they realized they were trapped in a cycle. They wanted to reconnect but didn't know how. There was no longer a desire to make love. The sexual act had turned into a burden, a demand neither of them could bear anymore. Their relationship was becoming a distant memory of what had once been light and happy.

The distance between them seemed insurmountable. The following days passed in silence, with few words and many gestures of avoidance. Isadora no longer knew what to do. She could no longer accept continuing with something that no longer fulfilled her, but at the same time, she couldn't break the bond that still existed with Daniel.

Their relationship began to stretch over long days without connection, without passion. What was once a marriage now felt like a lifeless coexistence. And both were being consumed by it in diverse ways.

Isadora wondered if things could ever go back to the way they were, but deep down, she knew something profound had changed. And, as difficult as it was, that transformation was irreversible.

The following years were marked by tireless attempts to rescue what once had been the heart of their relationship. Isadora and Daniel were together, but emotional distances and frustrations began to weigh on both. Their relationship had turned into a silent battle where love stayed, but desire and complicity had disappeared.

Feeling increasingly unable to meet Isadora's expectations, Daniel began seeking help. He consulted doctors, therapists, and specialists. He tried everything to understand what was happening with his body and mind. The answers, however, were vague. The illness he faced, the one that affected his ability to connect emotionally and physically, had no cure. Worse still, the number of cases was so small that doctors doubted whether it was worth pursuing further research.

He felt powerless. The conversations in consultations often left him more confused. There were no easy solutions. And as the months passed, Daniel began sinking into a silent depression. His self-image deteriorated, and the emptiness he felt inside seemed impossible to fill.

Attempts to reignite the flame in his relationship with Isadora proved increasingly frustrating. He tried various approaches, but nothing seemed to work. His gestures were often made in desperation, trying to adapt to what he believed were his wife's needs. Sometimes, he even allowed himself to explore new ways to get closer to her, trying to find a way to reconnect. But everything seemed empty, and the distance between them only grew.

Isadora, for her part, tried to be understanding, but the emotional exhaustion was beginning to weigh heavily. She knew how hard Daniel was trying, but her own frustration grew. The conversations that had once been open and honest turned into empty dialogues without answers. She no longer found pleasure or satisfaction in his gestures, which made her feel guilty and confused. The expectations she had, what she genuinely wanted from the relationship, seemed increasingly out of reach.

The therapies they tried together did not have the expected effect. The promises of change, the renewed hopes at each appointment, faded when they returned home to the same routine of emotional loneliness. Each failed attempt sank the relationship deeper, and both began to realize that something was broken beyond repair.

Isadora was now torn between the love she still felt for Daniel and the reality of a marriage that no longer fulfilled her. She tried to be patient, but her attempts to find happiness collided with the emptiness she felt. Daniel, on the other hand, did his best to be the husband she deserved, but the illness and emotional problems were taking over him in ways he no longer knew how to control.

During one of those silent periods, Isadora found herself thinking about what she might have done differently, what she had lost over the years. She wondered if there was still something she could do to save the relationship, but the truth was that with each passing day, she felt further from the woman she had been before all this. She no longer knew what she wanted, but she knew that what she was living was not enough for the woman she wanted to be.

And then, with time, the pain of emotional exhaustion took over. She no longer knew how to continue being the devoted wife and the woman he expected. She no longer knew how to love in a way that was true to herself. And in the end, that was what was really missing: being true to herself.

The silence between them was like an invisible wall that grew thicker each day, suffocating everything that was once light, laughter, and affection. Isadora felt that distance not only in the space between their bodies but in the absence of the soul that once inhabited their marriage. And that hurt more than any words could express.

She found herself watching Daniel in quiet moments, searching for the man who had once been her safe harbour, her best friend. But all she saw were shadows—shadows of a wounded man, lost, desperately trying to hold onto something he no longer knew if it even existed.

Inside, Isadora felt a growing emptiness, as if she were watching her own life slip through her fingers, powerless to hold on. She wanted to cry, but the tears never came; it was a silent anguish, a muted scream with no voice.

Daniel, for his part, fought invisible ghosts that consumed him from within. Jealousy, guilt, the shame of not being enough for the woman he loved—all of it slowly ate him away. He became a prisoner of his own feelings, and with every failed attempt to rise again, the weight of defeat grew heavier.

He wanted to speak, to explain, to ask forgiveness for not being the man Isadora needed at that moment, but words escaped him. How could he express pain without a name? How could he share a battle fought alone in the silence of his mind?

In their gazes, there was a contained storm, a mutual pain no one dared to face. It was as if they both carried a secret too heavy to share, a burden growing and threatening to crush what was left of the love between them.

Isadora felt her heart shatter into tiny pieces scattered on the invisible floor of the room they shared but no longer met in. Every attempt to draw close was a risk, a step into the darkness where she didn't know if she would find comfort or rejection.

She knew he suffered, and that made her want to be strong for both. But that strength also drained her until nothing was left but the exhaustion of trying to hold on to something that might be falling apart for good.

His eyes, once full of life and passion, now seemed lost, distant, as if Daniel's soul were slowly fading away. And Isadora wept inside, for his pain, for their pain, for the hope that stubbornly refused to die.

On lonely nights, when the house fell silent, Isadora allowed herself to cry softly, feeling the invisible hand of loneliness squeeze her chest. She remembered the happy times, those nights when love was light when the future seemed an open and promising path.

But now, all of that felt like a distant dream, a story from another life. And she wondered if they would ever find that path again or if they were doomed to walk separate roads, each carrying their own scars.

Daniel, despite his pain, couldn't escape the love he felt for Isadora. It was a trembling flame, a fragile light amid the darkness consuming him. And that tormented him—wanting to love but unable to find the strength to reconnect.

He searched for answers that never came, doctors with no cure, therapies that promised but did not deliver. Frustration became a wall that separated them, an invisible barrier that seemed to grow with every failed attempt.

Isadora tried to understand, to forgive, to keep the flame of love alive, but emotional exhaustion made her want to give up everything. And the fear of losing Daniel, of losing herself, paralyzed her.

Their relationship became a minefield of unspoken feelings, avoided gestures, silences heavy with pain. They were together but alone. Close, but distant. And that hurt more than any fight, more than any physical separation.

She knew she loved that man, that her love was true, but she no longer knew how to love him in a way that wouldn't destroy her. She no longer knew how to save a relationship that, to her eyes, seemed doomed.

Nights became silent witnesses to tears that slid down their cheeks, hidden from the other's eyes, kept as a painful secret. Each one carried a silent plea for help, for understanding, for a miracle.

Isadora felt torn between hope and resignation. She wanted to believe they could find each other again, but with each passing day, that hope seemed more fragile, like a crystal about to break.

Daniel, in his solitude, sought strength in the memory of happy moments, the scent of Isadora's hair, the touch of hands that once gave him life. It was all he had left, memories that both hurt and comforted.

And so, amid silent tears and stifled sighs, Isadora and Daniel kept living that broken love in the painful hope that, one day, the light could shine on them again.

Because, despite everything, their love still existed—not perfect, not whole, but real. And that was what, in the end, kept them there: the invisible strength of a feeling that no pain could erase.

85

Chapter 14
The Silent Destruction

Each passing day felt harder for Daniel. He saw Isadora's gaze grow more distant, her expression increasingly clouded with a sadness he didn't know how to heal. Their conversations became shorter, their laughter rarer, and their touch—once natural and intimate—had now become an almost uncomfortable formality. He felt the weight of his impotence growing, like an invisible burden nesting in his chest, tightening, suffocating, making the air harder to breathe.

The reflection of his pain was mirrored in Isadora. When he looked at her, he didn't just see the woman he loved—he saw a woman slowly saying goodbye to her own happiness. He knew she didn't want him to notice, but there was no way to hide the truth. Her eyes, now empty and distant, were the silent scream of someone who no longer found meaning in what their relationship had become.

Daniel tried everything to change the situation, but each attempt only pushed Isadora further away. He knew she needed something he couldn't offer. Frustration mixed with shame, and that made him retreat even deeper into himself, avoiding any interaction that might further expose his vulnerability—not just with Isadora, but with himself.

As the days dragged on, Daniel felt as though he were sinking into a deep, dark pit. Every failed attempt, every frustrated gesture, was like a stone being thrown into the bottom of that abyss, making the pain heavier and more unbearable. He constantly asked himself: Why can't I be the man she deserves? Why am I failing?

Doctors had told him his condition was rare, almost impossible to treat. He knew that, but words weren't enough to soothe the pain of watching Isadora grow more distant, more silent. He watched her from afar, trying to understand what he could do to turn things around. But what tore him apart the most was realizing that, in trying to be strong, he was destroying himself from the inside out.

Isadora, in turn, was trying to understand as well. She felt a growing compassion for him but also a growing frustration with herself. The love was still there, but the need to be seen, to be loved, to be touched and desired was becoming something painful and distant. She felt Daniel's pain, but at the same time, she felt the pain of her own emotional solitude. And that consumed her little by little, like a flame that no longer had fuel to keep burning.

She saw Daniel getting lost in his own guilt, and that broke her even more. When he spoke of his frustrations and limitations, Isadora felt her own soul fracture into smaller and smaller pieces. She tried to be strong but no longer knew what to do. She was torn between the love she still had for him and the need to be happy—to be seen, to be wanted in a way she could no longer find at his side.

The nights had grown long and silent. There were no more sweet words, no more promises of better days. Only the heavy silence that settled between them—an invisible barrier neither dared to break. Daniel tried to be the best husband he could be, but all he could see reflected on him was his own incapacity. He knew Isadora deserved more, but he also knew he had nothing left to give.

Worst of all was the constant feeling of helplessness. He wanted to go back in time, to be the man she still saw at the beginning—the man who made her laugh, who made her feel loved. But now that seemed so far away, like a fading memory, a blurred image he could no longer reach. And Isadora, by his side, seemed to be doing the same, trying to hold on to a love that was no longer the same.

Daniel's pain was not just in the lack of physical connection but in the emotional destruction unfolding before him. He was losing the woman he loved, and he no longer knew how to save her. He no longer knew how to save himself.

Each day felt like a new blow, a fresh reminder of his failure. He became more withdrawn, more closed off as if the only safe place left were within his own pain. And Isadora, despite all her efforts, was also getting lost. She felt that as Daniel destroyed himself, she too was falling apart—without knowing where to go, without knowing what to do. And so, their relationship, once a vibrant love story, was becoming a shadow of what it once was.

Each passing day grew heavier for Daniel. He saw Isadora's gaze drift further away, her expression increasingly burdened by a sadness he had no way to heal. Conversations shortened, laughter became rare, and the touch that was once natural and intimate between them had transformed into an almost uncomfortable formality. He felt the weight of his impotence grow—a silent burden nesting in his chest, tightening, suffocating, making the air harder to breathe.

Daniel spent long hours alone in silence, struggling to understand where everything began to crumble. It was as if he stood before a labyrinth with no exit; every attempt to find a path only left him more lost. He wondered if there was some moment, some word, some gesture he could have made to hold Isadora's hand more firmly.

Guilt was a poison coursing through his veins. He felt trapped by his own helplessness, a man desperate to be strong but slowly unravelling from within. Every time he reached out, her hand seemed to slip away, as if Isadora belonged to a world he no longer had access to.

At night, lying awake staring at the ceiling, Daniel thought of the promises they had made, the future they had dreamed of—and a tight knot formed in his throat. The cheerful, confident, and secure man he once was dying slowly, buried beneath the weight of failure and despair.

He didn't want Isadora to suffer, but her pain reflected his own with brutal clarity. Her vacant, distant eyes were like a blade piercing his chest, cutting through his soul, and leaving behind a trail of hopelessness. Daniel wished he could take that sadness away from her as if he could absorb all the pain himself.

Deep down, he knew she needed something he could no longer give—and that knowledge was destroying him. The helplessness of not being able to heal, not being enough, led him to a place of solitude few dared to enter. A dark place where the silence roared.

He remembered all the times he tried to open his heart, to speak his feelings, but the words got lost in the air—as if afraid to hurt what little remained between them. The shame of being vulnerable made him shut down, hiding his pain behind walls of silence.

Every look Isadora cast at him felt like a silent verdict. He knew she was hurting too, but their mutual fear of confronting that shared pain only pushed them farther apart. It was a cruel game of emotional hide-and-seek with no winners.

Daniel began to avoid places that once belonged to both. The couch where they used to embrace, the kitchen where laughter filled the air and dinners were prepared, the bedroom where tenderness blossomed—now all seemed like strange territory, marked by the absence of what once was.

His mind tormented him, replaying every gesture and every word, searching desperately for the moment when love started to fade. But there was no clear answer—only a tangled mess of questions that choked him.

The fear of abandonment haunted him relentlessly. He dreaded the day Isadora might choose to leave; that absence could become permanent. The thought paralyzed him, trapping him deeper in his own labyrinth.

Daniel felt like he was sinking into a bottomless pit, where every effort to climb was met with new stones thrown on his back. Frustration mixed with profound sadness, making him a stranger to himself.

He found himself crying in secret, silent tears no one could see— because he didn't want Isadora to see him weak, lost, broken. His pride forced him to bear that unbearable burden alone.

In those moments of solitude, Daniel longed for the embrace that never came, for the words that comfort, for the touch that heals. Yet he distanced himself, fearing rejection, fearing the pain that might consume them both.

He wished he could turn back time, undo mistakes that never even happened, and recover the lightness of days when love was the only certainty. But the past was an unreachable place, a distant dream that tormented him.

The anguish he felt transcended the physical—it was an internal battle consuming his very identity. He asked himself who that man in the mirror really was—a man who lost the courage to be happy, reduced to a shadow of what he used to be.

Daniel felt trapped in a body that no longer obeyed, a mind betraying him, emotions that left him too vulnerable to face the world. He wanted to be strong for Isadora, but he also needed to be strong for himself—and he didn't know how.

Hope was a thin thread, an extinguished flame he fought to keep alive. He clung to joyful memories, to small victories from the past, searching for a reason to keep fighting.

Sometimes, he thought Isadora deserved someone better, someone who could offer what he no longer could. That idea corroded him, deepening his feelings of uselessness and failure.

In her eyes, he saw the desire to leave, though the words were never spoken. That killed him slowly because he wanted to be her safe harbour, the refuge to which she could always return.

Daniel knew he couldn't control everything—that some things were beyond his reach—but he couldn't accept that love could be lost this way: silently, without a scream, without explanation.

Each night was a battle against his own ghosts, against the growing loneliness inside him. He fought not to succumb to despair, but the weight of reality made every day harder than the last.

He felt himself breaking, every effort to be strong consumed him a little more. And as he broke, he destroyed what remained of their relationship—a silent destruction no one else noticed.

The love that still lingered between them was suffocated by fear, pain, and the inability to find a way back. It made Daniel feel like a castaway stranded on a desert island, hopeless for rescue.

He wanted to be heard, understood, and accepted in his vulnerability—but the fear of rejection made him close off, retreat, distance himself. A vicious cycle of pain feeding itself.

Daniel felt time was against them that each day increased the distance, the silence, the pain—and he didn't know how to stop their love from slipping away forever.

Desperation clouded his thoughts, leaving him exhausted, confused, hopeless. He wanted to believe in a better future, but the shadow of silent destruction hung over them, threatening to extinguish every light.

He knew Isadora loved him, just as he loved her—but love alone sometimes wasn't enough to heal the wounds life had inflicted.

And so, between tears left unwept and words left unsaid, Daniel found himself trapped increasingly inside his own emotional prison, hoping—in vain—for a miracle that could save what seemed doomed.

CHAPTER 15
SILENCES THAT SCREAM

Time had turned Isadora and Daniel's home into delicate territory, where any word could spark a flame. The arguments had grown—not in volume but in the intensity of the silences. Daniel spoke more than ever, a desperate attempt to keep something alive, while Isadora, in contrast, grew quiet.

She listened. Always listened. But she didn't respond.

She would sit on the edge of the bed or wash the dishes in silence, eyes lost as if she were somewhere else entirely. It was her way of surviving: staying silent to avoid exploding, retreating to avoid completely dissolving.

Daniel, in turn, had thrown himself into an online support group formed by men with the same condition—an emotional and physical dysfunction without a name, without a cure, without sufficient research. Among advice from frustrated doctors and inconclusive articles, what appeared most often in the conversations was an alternative "cure": liberalism. The idea of allowing their partners to seek satisfaction with others, within the relationship.

They spoke of it with almost religious enthusiasm. They claimed that watching their wives with other men reawakened something dormant. That it reversed the symptoms. That desire returned, passion was reignited, and their bodies responded. Daniel read everything carefully, desperate for a solution.

But Isadora didn't want to hear it.

She didn't want to relive that. Not out of lack of desire or compassion but because she still carried the silent guilt from the last time. Even if it had been consensual. Even if Daniel had asked. Even if, for a few hours, she had felt alive like she hadn't in years.

For her, the issue wasn't the act itself. It was the abyss that remained after.

It wasn't easy to simply repeat it. There was something in her that resisted—something she called values, history, morality. It wasn't judgment. It was pain. The feeling that every step outside that line tore away another piece of herself.

Daniel tried to argue. He showed her the stories from the group and read excerpts from messages with a fragile, almost childlike enthusiasm.

"They say this is it, Isa… That this is what changes everything. That this is how they were cured, that desire came back..." he'd say, hollow-eyed, hoping for a response that never came.

Isadora looked at him in silence. Not anger. Not pity. Just a calm, impenetrable exhaustion. A wall built from years of accumulated pain and broken promises.

She didn't want to hurt anymore.

Didn't want to do something out of obligation disguised as freedom.

Because deep down, she knew it wasn't really a choice. It was desperation.

Daniel felt it. He knew she was there—but not really. That the love still existed but was tired. And that her silence—that dense, long silence—screamed louder than any argument.

It was that silence that destroyed him from the inside.

With every unspoken "no," every quiet withdrawal, Daniel felt smaller. Inadequate. Not just as a man but as a partner. He knew it was asking too much. But the fear of losing her, of losing them, made him persist.

"Isa, please, just think about it... It doesn't have to be now. Just... think," he murmured in an almost pleading tone.

She closed her eyes. Didn't respond.

And so, the days dragged on. With love still alive but surrounded by limits, guilt, and fear. The only thing growing was the abyss between them—fed by silence, by broken expectations, by incompatible desires.

And for the first time, both began to wonder whether love alone was enough to sustain two worlds that no longer touched.

Time had transformed Isadora and Daniel's home into a fragile territory where any word could spark a fire. The arguments had multiplied—not because their voices grew louder, but because of the intensity of the silences between them. Daniel spoke more than ever in a desperate attempt to keep something alive, while Isadora, in contrast, remained silent.

She listened. Always listened. But never responded.

She would sit on the edge of the bed or stand at the sink washing dishes in silence. Her eyes lost in a place far away. It was her way of surviving: staying quiet so she wouldn't explode, withdrawing so she wouldn't dissolve completely.

Daniel, meanwhile, had thrown himself headlong into an online support group formed by men with the same condition he suffered— a physical and emotional dysfunction without a name, without a cure, and without sufficient study. Between frustrated doctors' advice and inconclusive articles, the most common topic was an alleged "alternative cure": liberalism. The permission, within the relationship, for their partners to seek satisfaction elsewhere.

They spoke about it with an almost religious enthusiasm. They claimed that watching their wives with others reignited something dormant. That it reversed the symptoms. That desire returned, passion was rekindled, and the body responded. Daniel read everything carefully, desperate for a solution.

But Isadora didn't want to know.

She didn't want to relive that. Not for lack of desire or compassion but because she still carried the silent guilt of the last time. Even though it was consensual. Even though Daniel had asked for it. Even though, for a few hours, she had felt alive in a way she hadn't for years.

For her, the problem wasn't the act. It was the abyss that remained afterward.

It wasn't easy to just repeat it. There was something inside her that resisted—something she called values, history, morality. It wasn't judgment. It was pain. The feeling that every step beyond that limit was a piece of herself breaking apart.

Daniel tried to argue. He showed her the men's stories from the group and read excerpts of messages with a fragile, almost childish excitement.

"They say that's it, Isa… That's what changes everything. That's how they managed to heal, how desire came back…" he said, eyes sunken, waiting for an answer that never came.

Isadora looked at him silently. Neither angry nor pitying. Just a calm, impenetrable weariness. A wall built from years of accumulated pain and broken promises.

She didn't want to hurt anymore.

She didn't want to do something out of obligation disguised as freedom.

Because she knew that, in the end, it wasn't a choice. It was desperation.

Daniel felt it. He knew she was there, but not there. That love still existed, but was tired. And that her silence—that dense, long silence— screamed louder than any argument.

It was this silence that destroyed him from the inside.

With every unspoken "no," with every veiled distancing, Daniel felt smaller. Incapable. Not only as a man but as a partner. He knew he was asking too much. But the fear of losing her, of losing them, made him persist.

"Isa, please, think... It doesn't have to be now. Just... think," he murmured in an almost pleading tone.

She closed her eyes. She didn't respond.

And so, the days dragged on. With a love still alive but surrounded by limits, guilt, and fears. The only thing growing was the abyss between them—fed by silences, by shattered expectations, by incompatible desires.

And, for the first time, both began to wonder if love alone was enough to sustain two worlds that no longer touched.

Daniel felt the weight of each silence like a stone in his chest. It was a deafening quiet, an absence so profound it screamed through the walls of their home. The space between them was no longer filled with words but with a void that swallowed hope.

His nights were restless. He replayed every conversation, every glance, every missed opportunity to reach Isadora's heart. The helplessness clawed at him relentlessly.

He wanted to scream, to beg, to cry—but his voice caught in his throat. Vulnerability was a foreign language he struggled to speak.

Daniel's mind was a battlefield of contradictory emotions. Love fought alongside despair; hope wrestled with resignation.

He felt a deep sadness for the man he was becoming—a man who was losing not only his wife but himself.

Isadora's silence was not indifference. Daniel knew that. It was a fortress built from pain, fear, and exhaustion.

Sometimes, he caught a flicker of the woman he once knew in her eyes. A spark that reminded him of their early days, of laughter and warmth. But it was quickly swallowed by the shadows.

Daniel longed to break through that wall, but every attempt pushed her further away.

He wondered if there was a limit to love's endurance—if some wounds were too deep to heal.

He remembered how she used to smile so freely, how her laughter used to light up the room. Now, those moments felt like distant memories, fragile and fading.

Daniel feared the silence was a sign of surrender—that Isadora was giving up on them.

And that fear was a torment worse than any physical pain.

For Isadora, the silence was a shield and a prison.

She was trapped between her love for Daniel and the pain that love was causing her.

She feared that speaking might unleash storms she wasn't ready to face.

Her heart was heavy with guilt—guilt for wanting to hold onto herself, even if that meant holding Daniel at a distance.

She felt torn between loyalty and survival.

Isadora's days were marked by quiet battles fought in the corners of her mind.

She longed for connection but feared vulnerability.

She wished for understanding but braced for disappointment.

Her silence was not a lack of feeling but an ocean of unspoken words and emotions.

Sometimes, she wept alone, mourning the loss of what once was.

Other times, she felt numb, as if emotions had fled, leaving a hollow space behind.

Isadora wondered if love could survive this deep a fracture.

She questioned whether they could rebuild on foundations so shaken.

Yet, despite everything, a fragile thread of hope stayed.

She held onto the belief that love, even wounded, could find a way.

Daniel and Isadora were two souls caught in a tempest of silence and sorrow.

Their love was evaluated beyond limits they never imagined.

The silences between them were not empty but charged with meaning—pain, longing, fear, and fragile hope.

And within those silences, both screamed in ways no one could hear.

The question lingered: would their love be strong enough to break the silence, or would it be swallowed by it forever?

CHAPTER 16
ALMOST FRIENDS

Time didn't cause an explosion. It simply extinguished, little by little, what once burned.

Daniel and Isadora still lived together. Still shared the same roof, the same breakfast, the same bed. But it was as if a thick, invisible glass stood between them. They slept side by side without touching. They spoke about bills, about groceries, about their son's medicine. But they no longer spoke about themselves.

There were no more fights. Only silence.

And that was the worst symptom.

It was the polite silence of those who had grown used to the absence of connection. The comfortable silence of those who avoid conflict because they know there's no strength left to rebuild. It didn't hurt like before—and that was the saddest part.

Isadora went through her days like someone walking through the fog: functional, efficient, present. But she had lost her spark. The intense woman, full of questions, desires, and longings—was now just performing tasks. As if merely passing through her own life.

Daniel saw all of it.

And suffered twice as much.

Because he knew the problem wasn't her. It was him. Or it was the us. A construction that had emptied over time and, no matter how much they tried to rebuild, no longer had a solid foundation to sustain what they once dreamed.

He tried not to show it, but every gesture of hers hurt him. The automatic affection, the kiss on the forehead, the "goodnight" without warmth. They had started treating each other with distant kindness, like good coworkers. There were no screams, no betrayals, no dramatic scenes. Just the quiet realization that they were no longer lovers. They were logistical partners. Co-pilots in a routine.

She made dinner.

He washed the dishes.

She put their son to bed. He tidied up the living room.

They talked about the weather, school, inflation.

And they forgot — or pretended to forget — that once they had been everything to each other.

Isadora began to avoid any intimate touch. It wasn't rejection — it was self-preservation.

She was afraid of what her body might say that her heart no longer confirmed.

And Daniel, in turn, stopped trying.

With each of her withdrawals, a piece of him withdrew too.

And so, little by little, they became just good friends sharing responsibilities.

No one slammed the door.

No one announced the end.

But the end already lived there.

And they, like so many couples, learned to live with it as if it were just another piece of furniture.

Sometimes, one would look at the other a little longer than necessary as if trying to remember when everything had been different. But they would soon look away.

It was easier that way.

And the most painful part was knowing that, despite everything, they still loved each other.

But there are things that love alone cannot heal.

Isadora woke before sunrise that Saturday.

The room still dark, Daniel asleep beside her, breathing deeply. Their son in the other room, dreaming his light, innocent dreams.

And she, there, with her chest pounding — like someone standing at the edge of a cliff.

But it wasn't fear. It was a decision.

Months of silence.

Months trying to forget what she felt, trying to respect what she thought was right.

She had carried guilt like a virtue. Avoided life for fear of losing herself.

But she was already lost.

She realized she could no longer deny what pulsed inside her.

It wasn't just desire.

It was the need to reconnect with the woman she had forgotten amidst so many roles: mother, wife, caregiver, warrior.

Isadora needed to remember who she was before she had to be everything for everyone.

She called Daniel.

His voice, still sleepy, came from the other end of the line.

— Is everything okay? — he asked.

— Yeah. I just wanted to say that today… I'm going out. With someone.

Silence.

Daniel didn't respond right away. And she didn't explain.

For the first time, she didn't ask for permission or give excuses. She just informed him.

He finally took a deep breath.

— I understand. Take care.

Isadora hung up.

Her hand trembled, but her heart was steady.

That night, she wore what she never dared to wear.

A fitted black dress, bold perfume, hair down.

For the first time, she dressed for herself — not to be accepted.

She looked in the mirror and saw a glow on her skin. Not from makeup but from freedom.

She met Gabriel at a discreet bar.

That same smile of his, now without expectation, just presence.

— You look different — he said.

— I'm alive — she replied, and they toasted with red wine.

It didn't take long.

Their eyes said what words didn't need to.

They went to a nearby hotel, where the outside world ceased to exist.

It wasn't just sex.

It was an expression of something deeper.

Touches full of hunger and surrender.

Laughter between kisses.

A body saying everything the soul had been choking on for so long.

She no longer compared herself.

She didn't think of Daniel.

Not the past.

Not the future.

In those hours, Isadora gave herself permission to be a woman.

Whole. Desired. Desiring.

And for the first time in a long time, she felt no guilt.

Only feeling.

Isadora came home with a tired body and a restless heart.

It wasn't guilt. It was something more complex.

A mix of relief and doubt, pleasure, and fear.

She took off her shoes at the door.

Walked slowly to the bathroom.

The cold light of the mirror reflected a different woman.

Still herself — but now whole.

There was a new steadiness in her eyes, a restless peace, like someone who knows something big has shifted inside.

She showered without hurry, washing the scent of the other off her skin — not out of regret, but so she could face Daniel honestly.

She sat on the living room sofa with a glass of wine.

The silence of the early morning wrapped around her, and for the first time, she didn't feel empty inside it.

Isadora didn't want to be an unfaithful wife.

She didn't want to live in hiding.

But she also didn't want to lose herself again.

For the first time in her life, she knew exactly what she wanted: freedom with truth.

She wasn't looking for another love.

She was trying to find her own again.

The next morning, she woke before everyone.

Made breakfast.

Prepared pancakes for her son.

Read the news on her phone as if returning to the world after a deep dive.

Daniel watched her from a distance, trying to decipher the new light in her movements.

He didn't ask.

And she didn't tell him.

Not yet.

But inside her, something was already decided:

She would never again give up who she was just to fit into a role that was too small.

And she knew that if Daniel wanted to stay by her side, they would have to relearn everything.

From the beginning.

Isadora began to walk differently.

Nothing ostentatious — no high heels, no red lipstick.

But there was a lightness in her step that seemed to say, quietly: I belong to myself.

Anyone looking from the outside wouldn't know exactly what had changed, but they could feel it.

She woke early, took long showers, applied lotion to her body as if caressing herself with time and care.

She cooked while listening to music, danced alone while the coffee brewed, and smiled more — not to please anyone, but because something inside her had finally awakened.

Daniel saw it, felt it, but didn't know how to respond.

He tried to stay close but always seemed one step behind. And she, without meaning to, kept stepping forward.

They no longer fought like before.

No yelling, no accusations, no tears.

But also, no warmth.

Their intimacy was now limited to everyday coordination: groceries, their son's homework, monthly bills.

They did everything together — like good friends. Good partners. Good parents.

But no longer a couple.

Isadora felt it in every lukewarm touch, every kiss without hunger.

And it hurt — not because of the ending itself, but out of fear of starting over, alone.

But she also knew: she could no longer dim herself just to preserve the appearance of a stable life.

One night, Daniel tried to reach out.

He caressed her back in bed, kissed her neck.

She didn't pull away. But she didn't open either.

She let him try. And with pain, she felt how far he was from himself.

His gestures came more from guilt than desire, more from effort than connection.

It ended with a sigh from him and silence from her.

— Are you okay? — he asked.

— I am — she replied. But they both knew she wasn't.

The following week, she returned to therapy.

Started writing regularly.

Not in the hidden notebook from before, but in a new journal, left in plain sight.

A phrase on the first page:

"I'm never going back to the place where I forgot myself."

It was the beginning of her return to her own truth.

The silence between Daniel and Isadora had become a constant presence, almost tangible—a shadow that followed them wherever they went inside that house. Sometimes, he would sit in the living room staring into nothingness while she tidied the kitchen, both occupied but trapped in worlds that no longer met.

There was a strange comfort in that distance. They didn't have to hurt each other or explain themselves. They avoided pain because it had become routine.

Isadora looked at Daniel and saw the man she once loved, but she also saw the invisible barrier that time and fear had built. It was a wall made of absences, unspoken words, lonely nights sharing the same space.

They talked—or rather, exchanged information—about what was necessary, not what mattered.

Daniel said, "Benjamin has a fever today. Did you make sure he took his medicine?"

Isadora answered without looking in his eyes,

"I took care of it. Everything's fine."

Routine had replaced passion. Love had put on silence as a disguise.

It was a coexistence more like a rehearsed choreography. Neither dared to step out of rhythm so they wouldn't break the fragile balance of "almost friendship."

Both knew this comfort was a prison. Still, they preferred it to face the pain of confrontation.

There was an almost physical sadness in Daniel's gestures when he avoided holding Isadora's hand on the way to the bedroom or when he looked away after receiving a lukewarm, lifeless goodnight kiss.

Isadora, in turn, missed that touch that made her feel alive, but she could no longer offer it without feeling like she was betraying herself.

Days passed like pages of a sad book—without twists, without hope, just what was left of a story that began full of dreams.

They still laughed sometimes, but the laughter was small, restrained, disappearing quickly like smoke.

It was the friendship left over from love—a bond without depth but that sustained what remained of the family.

Daniel remembered the nights when the house was filled with conversations about plans, trips, promises. Now, those words had turned into murmurs from the past.

No matter how hard he tried, he couldn't find the key to reopen that closed door.

Isadora felt a tight knot in her chest when she saw Daniel hugging their son—a simple gesture of affection that reminded her how much they had once been one.

She was afraid of feeling too much, afraid that love would hurt even more.

So, she preferred to be rational, avoided confrontation, built walls to protect herself.

Daniel noticed this, and in his loneliest moments, he felt invisible—not because Isadora ignored him, but because they couldn't reach each other anymore.

The words that once held power now sounded empty, almost grotesque in their repetition.

Silence became the language of what couldn't be said, of what had no solution.

They stayed together, but no longer as a couple.

And this reality hurt them with the intensity of an open wound.

Isadora often wondered in her solitude if they would ever be able to look at each other again as lovers or if they were destined for this "almost friends" coexistence.

Daniel, inside, wept for the vibrant woman he once knew—the woman who now hid behind a polite smile and a distant gaze.

Sometimes, he tried to get closer, but he always felt her body stiffen as if fearing a touch that could shatter the little they had left.

She wanted to believe there was still something there, but the fear of rejection was stronger than the desire to try.

It was a cruel paradox: love was there, but they no longer knew how to love it.

Deep down, both knew change was inevitable.

They couldn't keep living in that house as strangers who shared space and responsibilities.

But they were also afraid of the emptiness that an end would bring.

Isadora wrote in her diary to give voice to what she couldn't say. Sometimes, the words came like tears—painful, sincere, revealing.

And Daniel, unknowingly, was the protagonist of every page written.

There was a silent anguish in both—a had desire and a bitter resignation.

They were trapped between who they were, who they are, and who they might become.

And in that "almost friends," there was a sadness deeper than any fight or argument.

It was the sadness of love lost, connection broken, intimacy evaporated.

Yet, even in this state, there was a faint seed of hope—a nearly forgotten wish to find themselves again, to rebuild, or at least to accept with peace what life had imposed on them.

In that scenario, they were survivors of a love that had changed shape.

And, someday, that transformation could open a path to something new.

CHAPTER 17
PERMISSION

Daniel closed the door slowly, like someone honouring a ritual.

He got dressed calmly, almost solemnly.

Backpack on his back, their son in hand, an excuse rehearsed: a walk in the park, pizza later.

Isadora hugged him gently before they left — not like a wife saying goodbye to her husband, but like a silent partner letting go.

He said nothing but looked into her and nodded.

He knew what was coming.

Isadora stepped back inside.

Alone, she stood still for a few minutes in the centre of the living room, her heart racing.

It was a new kind of freedom — conscious, negotiated, raw.

There was no betrayal.

But there was the risk of never being able to go back to what they had been.

She went to the bedroom.

Took off the black dress she had picked out hours earlier.

Put perfume behind her ears.

Slipped into a simple, lacy black lingerie.

She paid attention to every detail — not as an offering to someone else, but as a gesture of self-respect.

Gabriel arrived a few minutes later.

There was no rush. No shame.

It was a reunion of desires, not of justifications.

She opened the door with a shy but steady smile.

He stepped in with bright eyes, admiring her without hesitation.

— You look beautiful — he said.

She didn't reply.

She simply pulled him by the shirt, and the kiss that followed was the beginning of surrender without limits.

They were together for hours.

But now, with no urgency, no fear.

There were slow kisses, then wild ones.

Clothes falling like autumn leaves.

She gave herself fully — body, voice, gaze.

She had orgasms that came in waves, pulling from her layers she hadn't even known were there.

He adored her with devotion as if she were living art.

And this time, unlike the first, it wasn't just pent-up desire.

It was the exercise of freedom.

A kind of faith in her own pleasure.

At the end, lying naked beside him, sweaty, her hair sticking to her forehead, Isadora smiled.

A calm, almost childlike smile.

Gabriel stroked her back and kissed her shoulder.

She knew it wasn't love.

But it was truth.

And that was enough.

Isadora lay there for long minutes after Gabriel left.

The door still half-open, the sheets messy like a living painting of what they'd just experienced.

Her breath still uneven.

The smell of him, of her, of sex — all mixed in the air like a forbidden perfume she didn't want to erase.

She felt alive.

But not like someone waking from a coma.

It was something else.

Alive like someone who, finally, belongs to herself.

The body, still warm, pulsed as if it had remembered itself after years of slumber.

The skin glowed — not just from sweat, but from pleasure.

The skin whispered a secret: "I exist."

She walked naked through the house.

Poured herself a glass of water, smiled at her reflection in the mirror — messy hair, damp eyes, lips swollen from kisses.

There was no guilt.

No shame.

There was, instead, a silence full of answers.

The silence of someone who had found herself again.

She sat on the bed and picked up her phone.

Videos. Photos. Fragments of the night recorded not out of vanity but as testimony — a record of the woman she was when no one was watching.

She sent everything to Daniel, as they had agreed.

Right after, she wrote:

"It was intense. I'm okay. I feel whole. I need a shower."

There was nothing more to say.

She stepped into the shower and let the water run slowly over her.

Her body still responded with small contractions, vivid memories of that touch, that surrender.

Isadora closed her eyes and laughed softly to herself.

Not a loud laugh — an intimate one.

The laugh of someone who, at last, had seen herself.

It was more than orgasm.

It was belonging to herself.

It was no longer apologizing for who she was.

When she got out, she slipped into a light nightgown — not to entice, but because her body deserved tenderness even in what she wore.

She sat on the balcony with a glass of wine.

And there, between the night breeze and the music playing in the background, she whispered:

— Now, finally… me.

Isadora stayed there, still, feeling the wine slide down her palate. The warm taste heated more than her throat—it was a fire kindled from within, slow, and unhurried.

She closed her eyes and breathed deeply. For the first time in a long while, she felt in control of her own time, her own story.

She thought of Daniel. Not with sadness, nor anger. Only with a distant, almost familiar affection that no longer hurt.

What existed between them had changed, and that was an irreversible fact, but it didn't have to erase through what they had lived.

Isadora knew life wasn't made of certainties. It was made of meetings and farewells that left marks.

Marks that sometimes even healed.

She was no longer the woman who sacrificed herself out of fear of being left behind.

Now, she was someone who allowed herself to feel. Who accepted the complexity of her own desire.

The freedom she discovered that night was an extension of her truth—not an escape from it.

She felt a pang of longing. Not for routine but for the intimacy she had lost with Daniel.

But she didn't want that longing to become a cage.

She wanted it to be just a thin thread she could look at without getting tangled.

There, on the balcony, with the night whispering secrets, Isadora promised herself:

"I will never lose myself again just to find myself in others."

Her phone vibrated softly. It was a message from Daniel.

"I saw the videos. I'm happy for you. I hope you keep being this way."

She smiled. It wasn't a message of jealousy or blame but of respect.

It was the respect that still existed there, even if in different forms.

Isadora replied:

"Thank you. Today, I started to find myself again."

She lay back on the chair, eyes fixed on the starry sky.

She thought of Benjamin, her little boy, sleeping peacefully, unaware of the complexity of grown-ups.

He was the anchor during the storm. The unconditional love that demanded only to be.

She sighed, feeling a great tenderness swell inside her chest.

It was a quiet love but a powerful one.

Isadora no longer needed grand declarations to feel alive.

This moment of stillness, acceptance, and shared silence with herself was enough.

She remembered the days when fear paralyzed her, and she smiled quietly within.

Today, fear no longer ruled her.

She faced it with strength, acknowledging it but no longer letting it dictate her choices.

At that moment, she felt the call of life—not perfect life, but real life.

The one that carries pain, joy, uncertainties, and discoveries.

And it was hers.

Suddenly, her phone rang again.

It was a photo from Daniel—Benjamin smiling, his face lit by morning light.

She saved the image like a talisman.

A reminder that even amid change, love stayed.

A love that transformed, adapted, endured.

Isadora got up and walked to the bedroom.

She ran her hand along her skin, feeling every part of herself awake.

She no longer needed to rush to be whole.

She already was.

She knew the road ahead was uncertain, but now she wasn't afraid to walk it.

For the first time, she felt able to look in the mirror without judgment.

She knew the permission she had given herself that night was not just to be with another.

It was permission to be.

To live.

To love in all its forms.

Before sleeping, she wrote in her journal:

"Today, I took the first step to free myself. To exist in myself, before anything else."

She closed the notebook with a soft smile and turned off the light.

That night, Isadora slept with a light soul.

Knowing that, finally, she was on the right path—the way back to herself.

Chapter 18
She Returned Before He Did

Daniel entered slowly as if the silence of the house might scream a truth he still wasn't ready to hear.

Their son was already asleep, as planned.

And Isadora was in the kitchen, her back turned, stirring something in a pan — wearing a pale nightgown, freshly bathed skin, hair down, barefoot.

He stopped at the doorway and simply watched.

It was her.

But not quite.

Or, for the first time, it was the uncut version of a woman he had only ever known in fragments.

— Hungry? — she asked without turning, her voice calm. Almost ethereal.

— I am… — he replied in a whisper. But it wasn't food about which he was talking.

She turned slowly.

Her eyes calmer than he expected. Softer.

And in them was something that hurt him:

It wasn't guilt.

Nor an apology.

It was peace.

Isadora placed the plate on the table and sat across from him.

There was no rush.

No masks.

— Did you see everything? — she asked, steady.

He nodded. — I did.

She looked at him.

Not with arrogance, not with fear.

With the dignity of someone who had found herself.

Daniel said nothing for a while.

He picked up the fork, stirred the food.

Then he spoke, barely above a whisper:

— You looked happy.

Isadora swallowed hard.

But she didn't explain.

Didn't ask for forgiveness.

She simply said:

— I felt alive. I don't even know if it's about sex, Daniel.

It's about existing without feeling like I must ask for permission.

He nodded, chest tight.

Yes, there was jealousy.

There was pain, wounded pride.

But there was a cruel clarity: she had returned before he did.

While he was still trying to gather his pieces, she had already rebuilt herself.

— I don't know if I can keep up with you — he confessed, his eyes wet.

— I don't want to leave you behind — she said, placing her hand gently over his.

And in that touch, Daniel understood:

Love still existed.

But it was changing shape.

Changing structure.

Changing course.

After they ate in silence, Isadora turned off the lights, turned off the world — and led Daniel to the bedroom.

They lay there, face to face.

Their son asleep in the next room.

Time, in that space, moved differently.

And then he cried.

Silently.

Isadora held him.

Like someone embracing a man — but also the lost boy inside him.

They stayed like that for hours.

No sex.

No rush.

Only truth between their bodies.

And for the first time in a long while, Daniel slept in peace.

Morning light slipped softly through the cracks in the curtain, painting the room in golden silence.

Daniel woke before the alarm.

His body lighter.

His mind quieter.

But what truly woke him… was her presence.

Isadora, still asleep, her hair spread loosely over the pillow, breathed deeply.

Her lips slightly parted. Her skin still carried the scent of a fresh shower and the mysteries of the night before.

He watched her for a while.

As if it were the first time.

As if he were looking at something sacred and untouchable — and yet, so close.

And then she opened her eyes.

They smiled.

Without a word, their bodies met in the middle of the bed.

It wasn't rehearsed.

It was impulse. Desire. A hunger for all they had silenced for far too long.

Slow kisses, firm hands, old shivers returning as if they had never left.

Isadora smiled with her eyes closed.

There was something new in her — a glow, a lightness, a freedom almost wild.

And Daniel, by instinct or desperation, responded with the full intensity of someone who loves — and fears losing.

Before their son even woke up, they lived what they hadn't in a long time:

A moment just for them.

No guilt.

No rush.

No past weighing them down.

It was more than sex.

It was a reunion.

And when they finally lay side by side, breathless and smiling, Isadora turned to him and said, her eyes glowing:

— Thank you for not giving up on me.

He pulled her close, his face buried in her hair, and thought, without daring to say it aloud:

"You're the one who keeps me standing."

Daniel entered slowly as if the silence of the house might scream some truth he wasn't ready to hear.

Their son was already asleep, just as they had agreed.

Isadora was in the kitchen, her back turned, stirring something in a pot — wearing a light nightgown, skin still fresh from the bath, hair loose, barefoot.

He stopped in the doorway and just watched.

It was her. But she wasn't the same.

Or she was, finally, the uncut version of a woman he had only known in fragments.

"Are you hungry?" she asked without turning around, her voice calm, almost ethereal.

"I am…" he answered in a whisper. But it wasn't food about which he was talking.

She turned slowly. Her eyes were calmer than he expected. Softer. And there was something in them that hurt Daniel: it wasn't guilt. Nor an apology. It was peace.

Isadora placed the plate on the table and sat down across from him. There was no rush. No mask.

"Did you see everything?" she asked firmly.

He nodded. "I did."

She stared at him. Not with arrogance nor fear. With the dignity of someone who had found herself again.

Daniel said nothing for a while. He picked up his fork, stirred the food. Then he let out, in a fragile voice:

"You looked happy."

Isadora swallowed hard but did not explain.

She didn't ask for forgiveness.

She just said:

"I felt alive. I don't even know if it was about sex, Daniel. It's about existing without feeling like I must ask permission."

He nodded, his chest tight. There was jealousy, yes. Pain, wounded pride. But a cruel clarity: she had come back before him.

While he was still trying to piece himself together, she had already rebuilt herself.

"I don't know if I can keep up with you," he confessed, eyes glistening.

"I don't want to leave you behind," she said, placing her hand over his.

And there, in that touch, Daniel understood love still existed. But it was changing shape. Structure. Path.

After they ate in silence, Isadora turned off the lights, turned off the world — and pulled Daniel into the bedroom.

They lay facing each other. Their son slept in the next room. Time, in that space, was different.

And then he cried.

He cried silently.

Isadora held him. Like someone who embraces a man but also the lost boy inside him.

They stayed there for hours. No sex. No rush. Just truth between their bodies.

And for the first time in a long time, Daniel slept peacefully.

The sun timidly entered through the curtain cracks, painting the room with a soft golden light.

Daniel woke before the alarm. His body lighter. His mind less tormented. But what truly woke him was her presence.

Isadora, still asleep, hair spread across the pillow, breathing deeply. Lips slightly parted. Skin smelling of bath and the mysteries of the night before.

He looked at her for a long time as if it were the first time. As if he were in front of something sacred and untouchable — and yet, so close.

Then she opened her eyes.

They smiled.

Without a word, their bodies met in the middle of the bed.

It wasn't a rehearsed gesture. It was impulse. Desire. Hunger for everything they had silenced for too long.

Slow kisses, firm hands, old shivers returning as if they had never left.

Isadora smiled with her eyes closed. There was a new light in her. A lightness. An almost wild freedom.

And Daniel, by instinct or desperation, responded with all the intensity of someone who loves — and fears losing.

Before their son woke up, they lived a moment that they hadn't lived for a long time: a moment just for them, without guilt, without rush, without the weight of the past.

It was more than sex. It was reunion.

And when they finally lay side by side, breathless and smiling, Isadora turned to him and said, with a sparkle in her eyes:

"Thank you for not giving up on me."

He pulled her close, burying his face in her hair, and thought, without the courage to say it aloud:

"It's you who keeps me standing."

She felt the weight of those words even without hearing them and squeezed his hand as if wanting to engrave that moment forever.

There, in that silent house where their son slept peacefully next door, two hearts began to beat in a new rhythm.

It wasn't the end of a cycle but the beginning of another.

And despite the uncertainties, they knew the journey was worth every step, every tear, every moment.

Because, after all, love wasn't perfect — it was real.

And that, in that instant, was enough to begin again.

CHAPTER 19
THE LOVE THAT REMAINS

Five years passed.

Time, with its wrinkles and silences, shaped Isadora and Daniel's days into something rare: a life together full of flaws — yes — but also of surrender, of listening, of a kind of love only those who have fallen apart together know how to rebuild.

They lived as they could. As they knew how.

Through setbacks and reconnections, through a desire that visited occasionally, and a tenderness that never quite left.

Isadora learned how to laugh again.

How to dance through the house, even on Gray days.

Daniel learned to cope with the limits of his own body.

With what illness took — and, paradoxically, what it revealed: the urgency to love while he still could.

He diminished slowly.

His strength faded.

Doctor's visits became routine.

The nightstand filled with pills.

And still, every night without fail, he kissed her forehead before sleeping — even when his body ached, even when his soul felt heavy.

Until the very last day.

That morning, Isadora found him on the couch, a book open on his lap, a serene smile on his face.

Daniel's heart had stopped.

Silently.

Loyal to the end.

In the pocket of his shirt, folded in four, a handwritten note:

"If I go before you, I want you to know: my love for you was never about the body, the bed, or my health. I loved you with everything I had left. And even when I was barely anything, I was yours. Always. — D."

Isadora read it with trembling hands and a shattered heart.

She cried over everything she had swallowed over the years.

Then she got up slowly, walked to the bedroom, and looked at herself in the mirror.

She was still there:

The woman he loved.

The woman he allowed to be free.

The woman who now carried the love of two.

And in that moment, Isadora understood that sometimes, the end is also a beginning.

Isadora's sense of time seemed to live in another lifetime. Everything in her had shifted. Her skin, her gestures, the way she occupied space in the world. But most of all, the way she felt.

After Daniel's passing, her days carried a different sound. An echo. As if every footstep in the house still waited to hear his. As if the air was still filled with his breath.

Grief didn't crash in all at once. It settled like a sheet, slowly covering everything. Isadora slept with it and woke up with it. Some days, she couldn't get out of bed. And others, inexplicably, she smiled, remembering an old joke, a silly note he once left on the fridge.

She discovered that the love that stays is quiet. It asks for no proof, no witnesses. It simply lives inside you.

In the early months, she felt rage. At God, at life, at Daniel. Why hadn't he taken better care of himself? Why hadn't he fought harder against death? But then, she understood he had fought. In his way. With dignity. With love.

Isadora started rereading old letters. The notes. The emails they exchanged even during the hardest times. In each line, she rediscovered the man he had been. The man she almost lost but who came back just in time to say goodbye in peace.

There were days she screamed alone. In the car, in the shower, into her pillow. Other times, she just let the tears fall during her morning coffee. Grief has its own routines.

Their son was growing. And with each passing day, he looked more like Daniel. The way he furrowed his brow, the way he listened to music, his love for black coffee without sugar. It was as if a part of Daniel had never left.

Isadora began talking to herself around the house. She'd comment on the recipes, on the weather, on laundry. As if Daniel were still in the next room, answering with that quiet smirk.

His shirts stayed in the closet. She couldn't bring herself to give them away. The scent still lingered. And on days of deep longing, she would sleep holding one.

There were moments when she thought about giving up. About leaving, moving abroad, erasing everything. But she didn't. Because there was a love there that held her up. A love that didn't need physical presence to be real.

She began to write. Journals, letters to him, short stories inspired by them. Writing became a bridge between their worlds.

One sleepless night, she wrote: "Today I didn't cry. I just felt you. Like wind brushing the back of my neck. That's enough."

She realized she was stronger than she had ever imagined. The pain hadn't broken her. It had carved her.

She remembered a phrase he used to say: "We only truly die when we're forgotten."

So, she kept his memory alive. She cooked his favourite meals on Sundays. She told their son the stories Daniel loved to tell. She planted daisies in the garden — the flowers, he said, looked like her laugh.

Friends tried to set her up with someone new. She declined. It wasn't time. It never would be.

Because some loves don't fade. They stay.

On a recent birthday, she made a chocolate cake and placed two candles on it. Her son found it odd. But she explained, "There are people we love forever. Even if we don't see them anymore."

Every now and then, she'd hear a song and remember the way he danced — out of rhythm, without shame. And she'd laugh. Loudly. Because remembering hurt. But it hurt beautifully.

Isadora went back to walking on the beach alone. But she always felt him beside her. As if his soul had dissolved into the waves, into the salty wind, into her steps.

On stormy nights, she'd still whisper, "Did you see that, love? What a beautiful rain."

Longing never left. It simply learned to live there — tucked into the folds of everyday life.

In the silences of the house, in their son's laughter, in the smell of morning coffee. Daniel was everywhere.

And Isadora kept going. One day at a time. Not out of bravery. But out of love.

The kind of love that stays even when everything else leaves. The kind that doesn't need eyes to be seen. Or hands to be touched.

The love that stays. Because it's made of soul.

And memory. And eternity.

And every time the night fell, and the world went quiet, Isadora would close her eyes and whisper words no one else could hear — but they were always for him.

Sometimes, she dreamed of Daniel. Not sick, not weak — but whole, smiling, reaching for her hand. And when she woke, she felt that it had really happened.

And in those moments, she knew that the love that stays is not just made of memory. It's made of an invisible presence.

One night, their son hugged her while she was reading and said, "Dad visits me in my dreams. He said he loves you very much." She simply smiled, eyes full of tears.

She began collecting small joys: a beautiful sunset, the scent of wet earth, a delightful book, a long hug. All of it, she silently dedicated to him.

Inside her chest, there was a space that would never be filled again. But around it, a garden had begun to bloom.

Isadora learned to live with absence the way one learns a new language: awkwardly, with effort, but full of meaning.

Sometimes, she wrote letters she would never send. Other times, she just talked to him in her head, like a prayer.

And whenever the ache in her chest grew too heavy, she'd place her hand over her heart and whisper to herself: "You loved. You were loved. No one can take that away."

Because, in the end, the love that stays doesn't need witnesses. It is enough on its own.

And Isadora, though still scarred, was also whole. A woman rebuilt through pain. And love.

The love that stays. Always.

CHAPTER 20
THE NEW BEGINNING

Isadora's grief was long, but time — as always — helped her find paths she never imagined possible.

The pain of losing Daniel would never leave her completely, but she learned to live with it, to carry it more gently.

There were days when the longing pressed hard on her chest, but she was no longer the woman she had been during the years of anguish and despair.

She had grown.

Evolved.

Healed in ways she hadn't foreseen.

It was on an ordinary day, when life finally was settling that she met Rodrigo.

He came like a breath of fresh air.

Rodrigo was everything she hadn't been looking for — and yet, somehow, he found her.

A man not only financially successful, but someone who looked at her with eyes that saw her fully.

Without rush.

Without expectations beyond the simple wish to see her happy.

He fell in love with Isadora deeply, without hesitation.

He treated her with care, with attention — and above all, with respect.

He wasn't trying to win her over with gifts or luxury;

He wanted to win her heart.

He wanted her to see in him something more than a man of status and wealth.

Rodrigo became a constant presence, both for her and for her son.

He genuinely cared for Isadora's boy, becoming actively involved in his life and helping build a home filled with love and support.

He gave Isadora the emotional stability for which she had longed.

And in her relationship with him, she no longer sought pleasure or validation elsewhere.

Rodrigo was kind, tender, and there — every day — ready to give her his best.

With time, Isadora allowed herself to rediscover pleasure.

She no longer needed to divide her soul among other bodies because Rodrigo had known how to love her completely — respecting her needs, desires, and dreams.

The pleasure she now felt was no longer a constant pursuit but a reflection of the love she had found — a love that made her feel valued, cared for, and, above all, free to be who she truly was.

Isadora had found happiness again.

She smiled more. Slept better. Laughed real laughs.

And when she looked at her son, she knew she was giving him a life full of love and opportunity.

She had finally healed from the scars life had left behind. Not that they had disappeared completely — but they no longer defined who she was.

She was Isadora. And now she knew she deserved to be happy. Truly.

But even as she gave herself entirely to this new love, something mysterious began to happen.

Sometimes, when Isadora was alone at home, she felt a gentle presence in the air.

As if something — or someone — was there, watching over her with affection.

And at certain moments, she felt a soft breeze pass by, like a silent greeting, a memory of Daniel.

And some days, when her little boy was playing around the house, he would begin talking about things that Isadora found strange — yet strangely comforting.

"Daddy is here again, Mummy. He's smiling at me."

Isadora, surprised, would watch him.

They spoke of Daniel with a familiarity only she could recognize.

He described the gestures, the smiles, the looks — and she knew he was seeing something she could not.

A spiritual presence. An energy.

"Are you seeing Daddy?" she asked, still in shock.

"Yes, Mummy, by the window. He's smiling. He says everything's okay."

At first, she thought it was just a child's imagination.

But over time, the little signs became more frequent.

He'd investigate corners of the room, toward the window, talking about something that was there — but invisible to her.

In the beginning, it gave her chills.

But soon, she grew used to it.

It was comforting.

There was one night, when Isadora was home alone, that she finally felt Daniel's presence in such a powerful way that she almost could touch it.

She was sitting on the sofa, eyes closed, trying to quiet the thoughts that tormented her.

And then, a soft breeze passed by — warm and peaceful — wrapping around her.

She opened her eyes and saw a gentle light filling the room, like an aurora glowing without blinding.

And there, in the middle of that light, she felt his presence.

Daniel was there.

Not as she had known him but as a glowing energy full of love.

There was no pain. No suffering. Only an immense peace embracing her.

And in that moment, she knew:

He was happy.

He was at peace.

He was watching over her in a way she could not fully understand — but she felt it in every part of her being.

When Rodrigo came home that night, Isadora was different.

Lighter. Serene.

She smiled at him — something she hadn't done fully in a long time.

"You're at peace, aren't you?" Rodrigo asked, noticing the calm in her face.

She nodded, unable to speak.

Because, at that moment, she knew Daniel was still with her.

Not physically — but in a deeper way.

He loved her in a way that transcended all earthly limits.

And somehow, she felt he was pleased to see her happy again — living in the present with someone who treated her gently and loved her for who she truly was.

And though the love she shared with Rodrigo was different, it was just as meaningful.

She didn't need anything more.

She was whole — because she had learned that true love never ends.

It simply transforms.

And Daniel, in some way, still loved her — not with a body, but with a soul.

Isadora and Rodrigo lived a life full of love.

Her son grew up in a home overflowing with affection, where the legacy of Daniel remained alive.

And Isadora, heart full and soul at peace, knew the future would be beautiful — because love, that eternal love, would always walk beside her.

And whenever she looked up at the sky, she saw one star shining brighter than the rest.

And she knew: that star was him.

Daniel.

Smiling at her.

Protecting her.

Loving her.

Always.

But after that day, the stars stopped shining.

The sky seemed to lose its light, and the wind no longer whispered in her ears.

Isadora felt Daniel's absence as if he had vanished completely — as if he had never existed.

That invisible warmth she used to feel, that gentle "I'm here" that touched the corners of the house, was gone.

Even when her son smiled at nothing, his eyes fixed on someone only he could see, Isadora could no longer feel Daniel's presence.

She didn't know if it was just imagination or something more.

But the nights grew longer.

The days, quieter.

And the peace she once felt faded into a silent melancholy she couldn't explain.

The love she had known with Daniel became a distant memory — like a scent that slowly disappears.

She no longer felt that light, that warmth, that invisible touch.

But deep inside, she knew he had never truly left.

The love he had given her — that immense, unwavering love — would remain forever inside her.

Isadora continued to live as she always had.

But in a different way.

She gave herself to the present, to the love Rodrigo offered her.

But even in all of that, the longing for Daniel never vanished.

It was like a puzzle piece in her life that, no matter how carefully replaced, never fit perfectly.

She smiled.

She loved again.

But there was always something that wouldn't fade.

And as the days passed, Daniel's memory — their moments together — would surface like a soft song, playing on the strings of her heart, reminding her of everything they had shared.

She knew he was still with her in some way.

But no longer in stars or gentle breezes.

Isadora smiled.

The smile of someone who, even though pain, had found peace.

She knew love doesn't fade — it transforms.

And even if silence now surrounded her, she knew her journey with Daniel had come full circle.

That he had loved her as she loved him.

And that he would always be a part of her, just as she would always be a part of him.

Life goes on.

So does love.

Even when the winds change and the stars disappear — love stays inside us. Immortal.

Isadora closed her eyes, feeling Daniel's presence in her heart.

No longer a shining light, no longer a physical presence — but a memory.

A love that transcended time and space.

She felt at peace, with a quiet smile on her lips.

The longing would always be a soft shadow.

But she knew, deep down, that Daniel would always be there.

In her heart.

And that was enough.

But that same night, alone in her bed, Isadora trembled. The breeze had vanished. The silence of absence filled the room with a cold emptiness. She touched her chest with a trembling hand—there was no longer that pulsing warmth, no more invisible electricity that once wrapped around her like a blanket. The spiritual world had withdrawn as if Daniel had, at last, left completely. As if he had fulfilled his silent promise to protect her... and now could finally rest.

She cried. Not the desperate weeping of mourning nor the tears of longing. It was a gentle, mature cry—like someone who understands that to love is also to let go. The true farewell doesn't happen at the grave but when the heart accepts that it's time to move on. And in that dawn, Isadora let him go. For the first time, fully.

The sun rose in golden hues that day. She walked to the porch barefoot, feeling the cool, solid wood beneath her feet. The world was still there. Life called her with its sweet, earthy imperfection. Isadora closed her eyes and took a deep breath. For the first time in years, the air was just air—no hidden messages, no signs from beyond. And strangely, that was comforting.

Later, when Rodrigo found her sitting in the garden, her gaze lost among the flowers, he embraced her from behind without saying a word. And she melted into his arms. It wasn't betrayal to love again. It wasn't disloyal to Daniel. It was simply being human. Rodrigo kissed the back of her neck with ancient tenderness, and she cried again—not from sadness. She cried because she was alive. Because she could still feel.

That night, she gave herself to Rodrigo with a new intensity. There were no more ghosts between them. No longer did another name echo across her skin. She was whole. Her moans no longer came from a place of forgetting but from the pleasure of being exactly where she was meant to be. Her body was a temple once more, and Rodrigo a devotee who adored her with reverence. He looked into her eyes the entire time, and she, unflinching, met his gaze with her soul laid bare.

"I love you," he said, as though for the first time.

"I love you too," she answered, with the certainty of someone who finally believes it.

And in that moment, as they made love under the quiet roof of their home, Isadora felt Daniel smiling somewhere far away. Not with jealousy. Not with pain. But with the lightness of someone who knows his mission is complete. He had been the love that taught. Rodrigo was the love that would remain.

In the following days, Isadora began to write. Every evening, with her son playing nearby, she let the words pour out like a reborn fountain. She wrote letters to Daniel—not to send them, but to eternalize him. Each line was a thread of affection woven with gratitude. And at the end of each letter, she signed with a quiet gesture: "With love, always. Isa."

One afternoon, her son brought her a drawing: three figures. A smiling woman, a man holding her hand... and another, in the background, with blue wings, watching over them. Isadora smiled, tears welling in her eyes.

"Who's the one with wings, sweetheart?"

"That's Daddy. He said he's like an angel now, but it's okay. He takes care of us from far away."

She pressed her son against her chest and, for a moment, felt that breeze again—not in the air, but inside her. As if longing had become part of her blood. A silent presence that no longer hurt—only stayed.

And so, Isadora moved forward. Her heart stretched between earth and sky, between what was and what would be. The past was no longer a weight. It became a root. Something that supported her without holding her down. And the present—with Rodrigo, with her son, with her new life made of simple gestures and full-hearted love—was the ripe fruit of that tree of deep affections.

She had learned, at last, that to love two men was not a sin. It was a rare gift. Daniel had been the fire that consumed her. Rodrigo, the ground that held her. Between the two, she was rebuilt. Whole. A woman again. Isadora.

And whenever the wind blew stronger, even without seeing a star in the sky, she closed her eyes and felt true love never leaves. It only changes form. And it stays, like a flame that does not burn—but warms—silent, eternal, divine.